THE MAKE-BELIEVE WIDOW

MATCHMAKING CHRONICLES
BOOK FOUR

DARCY BURKE

Zealous Quill Press

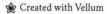 Created with Vellum

ADVANCED READER COPY

THE MAKE-BELIEVE WIDOW

Widower James Ludlow, Earl of Rotherham, attends a house party in search of a mother for his two daughters, and his primary requirement is that he doesn't fall in love. Having already given that emotion to his former wife without reciprocation, he prefers an unsentimental, mutually beneficial arrangement. However, he meets a charming widow with seemingly wonderful maternal instincts, and he can't ignore the sparks between them. Perhaps a little passion wouldn't be so unwelcome…

Everyone thinks Charlotte Dunthorpe is a widow, but she's only pretending to be. When her dear friend invites her to a matchmaking house party that isn't only for the purposes of marriage, Charlotte is tempted to indulge in a short liaison. Instead, the dashing and kind-hearted Rotherham offers her the chance for the family she always wanted. She must refuse or risk exposing her devastating secrets and ensuring the absolute ruin of all that she holds dear.

Don't miss the rest of the *Matchmaking Chronicles*!

Do you want to hear all the latest about me and my books? Sign up at <u>Reader Club newsletter</u> for members-only bonus content, advance notice of pre-orders, insider scoop, as well as contests and giveaways!

Care to share your love for my books with like-minded readers? Want to hang with me and see pictures of my cats (who doesn't!)? Then don't miss my exclusive Facebook groups!

Darcy's Duchesses for historical readers
Burke's Book Lovers for contemporary readers

Want more historical romance? Do you like your historical romance filled with passion and red hot chemistry? Join me and my author friends in the Facebook group, Historical Harlots, for exclusive giveaways, chat with amazing HistRom authors, and more!

CHAPTER 1

October 1803

*T*he moment Charlotte Dunthorpe stepped inside Blickton, the elegant and expansive country estate where her dear friend Cecilia, Lady Cosford resided, she knew she was completely out of place. Actually, her sense of unease had started when Lady Cosford's coach had arrived in Birmingham to bring her to the house party. All this was simply beyond Charlotte's normal life.

It was one thing to be friends and correspondents with a countess and another to accept an invitation to that countess's house party. Particularly a house party where the purpose was for attendees to form romantic associations—either temporary or permanent.

As a footman carried Charlotte's things upstairs to her room, Charlotte followed the butler to the drawing room, where Cecilia awaited her.

Despite Charlotte's anxiety, she was very much looking forward to seeing her friend. Her nervousness was caused by her surroundings and the coming week with people she'd never met. Would they look down on her? Find her lacking? Wonder why Cecilia had invited her?

Stepping over the threshold of the large, gorgeously appointed room decorated in rich golds and greens, with accents of blue and coral, Charlotte had to stop herself from looking wondrously about the space. Instead, she fixed on her hostess, who immediately rose from a settee and came toward her with a wide smile.

"Charlotte! It's been far too long!" Cecilia was so beautiful and elegant, her blonde hair always styled to perfection. She was also exceedingly kind and generous. They'd met at a salon in Birmingham five years ago and become instant friends. That Charlotte was a widow with a modest household and no family or connections hadn't mattered a whit to the countess.

They embraced for a long moment, and Charlotte couldn't help smiling. Cecilia's effusiveness and charm were ever-present, even in letters. To be together with her in person for the first time in—what, two years?—was a gift. It was the reason Charlotte had summoned her courage and accepted the invitation to an event she wasn't sure she wanted to attend.

Cecilia stepped back. "I'm so very glad you are here. I trust your journey was pleasant?"

"Your coach is exceedingly comfortable." It was, without question, the nicest and most well-sprung equipage Charlotte had ever had occasion to use. Granted, she'd rarely been in a vehicle these past ten years she'd been living in Birmingham. "Thank you again for allowing me to use it."

"I can't very well insist you attend my house party and not ensure you can get here," Cecilia declared with a laugh. "Come and sit with me for a few minutes. I'm so pleased that you're the first to arrive. This will give us some uninterrupted time together."

Charlotte followed her to the settee and sat down, her gaze moving about the room. "Blickton is beautiful," she said, trying to tamp down her unease. But why should she? Cecilia had been a good friend. "I confess I'm nervous to be here."

Cecilia's brow creased briefly. "Because of how I've arranged the party? You don't need to make a match. Just enjoy yourself and get to know everyone. I've invited a lovely array of people. You'll meet many who may even become friends."

"As we did," Charlotte said with a smile. "I almost didn't go that night we met—it was my first salon."

"It was, wasn't it? I'd forgotten. Well, it was my first one too, in Birmingham, that is. I'd only just arrived the day before to visit my godmother. And now look at us. I have treasured our friendship so much. Your letters never fail to brighten my day."

"I'm so glad. Yours do the same. I appreciate hearing of your children's antics." Charlotte had hoped to have children of her own, but now accepted that it wasn't likely to happen. Not unless she wanted a husband, and she wasn't entirely sure she did after ten years of independence. Or perhaps it was just that she'd gotten used to thinking she wouldn't have the chance to wed. But really, most of all, it was the lie she'd been living the past decade and the fact that she *couldn't* wed without risking everything.

And so, childless she would remain.

"I would have loved for you to meet them, but they aren't here this week as that would be inappropriate." Cecilia laughed. "The boys are at school, and the girls are visiting their grandmother. Since we are

3

discussing letters, in your last one, you mentioned young Hilda. What happened with her?"

Charlotte took in young women, some of whom were still really girls, in search of work. They were often alone in the world or trying not to be a burden on their families. Charlotte gave them the opportunity to train as maids, usually starting in the scullery and then learning other tasks. "She's still with me, though I expect she'll find a position in the next month or two. If she were a little older, I'd think she could even train as a lady's maid. My maid has shown her how to style hair and care for my wardrobe." Such as it was. Charlotte lived comfortably, but without excess.

"Indeed?" Cecilia cocked her head. "Do you think she'd mind leaving Birmingham? I've a need for an upstairs maid. And who knows, perhaps one day she'll become a lady's maid to one of my daughters."

Charlotte tried not to gape at her. "Truly?" Hilda was just sixteen, but she was bright and enthusiastic. "You'd be more than pleased with her."

"If she's coming from your household, I'll be lucky to have her. You've quite the reputation for training and placing excellent maidservants, according to my godmother." Cecilia's godmother had introduced them five years ago at that salon.

"I'm only trying to help some young women have a chance." Charlotte knew how close a woman was to complete disaster, particularly when she wasn't born into any kind of stability. Without a family or means, what could she do to protect and provide for herself?

"It's incredibly admirable," Cecilia said warmly. "Whenever you think Hilda is ready, I'd love for you to bring her here. If you don't mind visiting again. Then you can meet my children."

"I would enjoy that." Charlotte's nerves had settled slightly, but she was still anxious. "What sort of people have you invited to the party?" She didn't want to ask if anyone was like her, for she knew Cecilia paid no mind to the difference in their stations.

"People or gentlemen?" Cecilia asked with a mischievous look. She didn't wait for Charlotte to answer. "There are a few noblemen and noblewomen, but also several commoners, if that's what you're wondering. And zero Lord Manthorpes," she added conspiratorially.

Cecilia relaxed a bit more. She hadn't expected Lord Manthorpe to be here, as she knew that Cecilia didn't care for him. Which proved her good taste and intelligence. He was an overbearing, self-important arse, and the one person who could ruin Charlotte's life. She hoped to never clap eyes on him again.

"I can see that pleases you," Cecilia said. "While I may not know what Lord Manthorpe did to earn your disfavor, I can well imagine it involved him being a pompous knave."

"Pompous is an excellent description, as is knave." Even if Charlotte did encounter him someday, she had to hope he wouldn't recognize her. She, on the other hand, would forever recall his dark, piercing blue eyes as they surveyed her down his long nose.

"I can promise that the gentlemen attending the party are not of his ilk." Cecilia hesitated before adding, "Is there any chance you may wish to wed again?"

Again.

That simple word told such a huge lie. She'd come close to marriage, and indeed would have done if not for the untimely death of her betrothed—the day before the final banns were read. The situation in which she'd found herself had necessitated her immediate departure from the only home she'd ever known, Newark-on-Trent. And that was in some part due to Lord Manthorpe. He'd offered to make Charlotte his mistress the day after her betrothed— Manthorpe's cousin—had died. He'd been offensive and had tried to take liberties, but they'd thankfully been interrupted. Putting distance between herself and Manthorpe had been one of the reasons she'd left Newark-on-Trent and adopted a new identity.

Once she'd settled herself in Birmingham, she'd pretended as though she *had* been married. It had been a necessary fabrication, in the event that she was carrying a child, and even though there hadn't been a baby, she hadn't wanted to return to what she'd fled: the sadness of losing first her father and then her betrothed and the possibility that Manthorpe would force her to become his mistress. Furthermore, she'd established a wonderful life for herself and for those who depended on her, including her household and the young women they trained for domestic service.

Consequently, the lie had become the basis of her entire life. Correcting it now would be pointless as well as jeopardize everything she'd built. Nor did the lie harm anyone except Charlotte's sense of honor, which was why she tried to live her life above reproach and to be as kind and generous as she could.

"I don't think remarriage is for me," Charlotte said with a faint smile. "I'm quite content with my life in Birmingham."

"I do understand. In some ways, it's most enviable." Cecilia's eyes sparkled with curiosity. "Have you come to seek a liaison, then?"

"I don't know." Charlotte had engaged in just one affair in the past decade—if a single unforgettable night with a dashing Irishman could be considered an affair. "Mostly, I am here to see you."

"And I am so very glad." Cecilia patted her hand. "If you decide you'd like to…indulge, there will be several gentlemen here who would be amenable to that. I would say Lord Pritchard, who is twice widowed, and his children are nearly adults. Also, Sir Godwin Kemp, another widower with children. His charm can be slightly…aggressive, but he's a lovely fellow. I daresay Mr. Jacob Emerson may be your best option. He's just a couple of years older than you and has never been married. I am not sure if he's here to wed or not." Cecilia's expression turned pensive. "I'm also not certain if Lord Audlington is here to find a wife or engage in one of his famed liaisons—I do think he's tried to leave his rakish reputation behind."

Goodness, there were several choices, it seemed. Not that Charlotte was looking for that.

The butler appeared in the doorway. "Lady Cosgrove, another guest has arrived. May I present Lord Rotherham?"

A gentlemen stepped into the room, and immediately, the air around Charlotte changed. It thickened and heated, as if she'd stepped outside into a hot, still summer day where the sun warmed every shadowed place, even those best kept hidden.

"I hope I'm not intruding, Lady Cosgrove," the gentleman said with a smile that could only be described as wickedly alluring. His eyes, round and perhaps green, though it was hard to be certain at this distance, seemed to smile too. Indeed, his entire face, from his wide forehead to his jutted chin with its slight cleft, lit with cheer, making her think he must be a regularly happy person.

"Not at all, Roth. Do come and meet my friend." Cecilia looked toward Charlotte. "This is the Earl of Rotherham, though we all call him Roth." Then she

7

moved her attention back to the earl. "Allow me to present my very dear friend, Mrs. Charlotte Dunthrope."

The magnificent earl walked toward them, his tall, athletic form moving with an easy, masculine grace. He bowed, his golden-blond hair shifting against his temple, before saying, "It is my esteemed pleasure to make your acquaintance, Mrs. Dunthorpe."

Charlotte wished she'd been standing so that he could take her hand. Though she was sitting, should she offer it? She wanted to. So that she could feel his bare fingers against hers.

Why hadn't Rotherham been on Cecilia's list of potential liaison partners?

Perhaps because he was only here to find a wife. That was a terrible pity.

Cecilia waved him toward a chair nearer to Charlotte. "Sit, if you would, Roth. Unless you're fatigued and wish to retire?"

"Not at all. I had a very good night's sleep at the Sheep and Dog in Lutterworth."

"Splendid, as we have a lovely dinner planned for this evening with dancing to follow." Cecilia turned to Charlotte. "Roth is well known for his dancing ability. You won't find a better partner."

How Charlotte loved to dance! Alas, she had little occasion to do so. When she did attend an assembly, she was typically ignored along with the wallflowers and spinsters. Which made sense because she was, in truth, a spinster.

He fixed her with his stunningly attractive eyes, which she could now confirm were green. Specifically, they were the color of a fir tree in the forest one might encounter on a Yule log hunt, which Charlotte hadn't participated in since she was a child. "I trust you'll save me a dance this evening, Mrs. Dunthorpe?"

"It would be my privilege, my lord."

"Roth, if you please." He flashed another smile, and Charlotte's heart, which had already sped when he walked into the room, ticked up its pace.

Charlotte noted the fine lines fanning from his eyes. He had to be at least five years older than the thirty she possessed. How had a man with his charm gone this long without marrying? Perhaps he didn't really want to, but now needed to submit to duty and provide an heir to his earldom.

"How do you know Lord and Lady Cosgrove?" he asked. "I don't think I've met you at any of their balls or soireés. I surely would have remembered you."

Charlotte allowed a half smile even as she narrowed her eyes at him skeptically. "As it happens, I have not been to any of their social events, nor have we met. I would have recalled a gentleman as flirtatious as you."

The earl laughed softly, almost with a tinge of embarrassment. "That is not typically how one would describe me. I only meant that you have a most memorable face." The faintest marks of pink rose along his sculpted cheekbones.

Charlotte would have apologized for causing him discomfort, but the butler came again to announce that more guests had arrived.

Cecilia stood. "I suppose it is time for me to step fully into my role as hostess." She gave Charlotte a warm smile. "I'm glad we had a few minutes alone. Please, both of you stay if you'd like. As the guests arrive, we'll get to know one another here. Then we'll play a game of introduction." She arched her brows with an anticipatory look before walking toward the butler.

Charlotte turned to the earl. "I should not have assumed you were flirting. My apologies."

"I might have been, subconsciously even. I'm afraid my skills have been somewhat neglected."

"Is that why you've come to the party?" Charlotte asked. "To hone them once more?" There was a slight flirtatious edge to her question. Perhaps she would sharpen her skills as well, for they were also quite decrepit.

He grinned. "Indeed, I have. I have been widowed five years, and it is time I consider remarriage."

He *was* a widower, then, and he was here to find a wife. Disappointment flashed through her. A brief, sparkling liaison with Roth would have far exceeded any expectation she'd possessed for this party.

"How long have you been widowed?" he asked.

"Ten years. I wasn't married long." How she hated lying. In truth, she was surprised at how difficult it felt in this particular moment after becoming so used to it over the past decade. She'd thought she was nearly immune to the feelings of shame and frustration—not because of what had happened ten years ago, but because of the position she was in as a woman. Because her choices had been almost nonexistent. She refused to feel regret for choosing a life of independence, comfort, and, most of all, safety. Her father had raised her to do what was best, both for herself and those around her. She'd striven to do exactly that.

The earl's handsome features creased with genuine concern as his gaze met and held hers. "I'm sorry you lost your husband so soon. And ten years is a long time to be alone. Unless... Do you have a child? I have two daughters."

Daughters! How lovely. While her life was undoubtedly easier because she hadn't conceived a child with Sidney, she sometimes wished she had. "I do not have children. I have been alone, but don't feel sorry for me. My life in Birmingham has been full and content."

"I'm glad for you," he said earnestly. "Since you're here, may I presume you've decided you no longer wish to be alone?"

Put like that, Charlotte wanted to say yes. She couldn't deny that she yearned for a companion—in every way. Not marriage, of course, but to spend a few nights in the arms of a man like Rotherham would not be unwelcome. "That remains to be seen," she answered coyly, because she had to. "But I am... open to the party's possibilities." That was sufficiently vague so that she could either entertain an affair or not.

His eyes danced with anticipation. "How splendid to hear."

Charlotte abruptly stood, desperate for some space to breathe. The earl had quite set her equilibrium off, and she needed to put it to rights.

He also got to his feet.

"Please excuse me, your—I mean, Roth." She inclined her head. "I think I must retreat to my chamber for a respite. I'll look forward to seeing you later."

He smoothly clasped her hand. "It's been my pleasure to make your acquaintance." Lifting her hand, he bent his head and pressed his lips to her knuckles.

The touch was slight and brief. It should barely have registered. Instead, the connection shot straight into the very depths of Charlotte with a distinct heat, a desire that made her want to invite him to join her respite.

What a shocking thought.

Except, wasn't that what this party was for?

CHAPTER 2

*J*ames Ludlow, ninth Earl of Rotherham, stood from the dining room table and moved with the others to the drawing room. At their host's gentle prodding, the gentlemen had kept their time over port short this evening since it was the first night of the party.

Roth hesitated a moment before entering the drawing room. He would normally look forward to this. He enjoyed dancing and immersing himself in a pleasant evening. And he'd been anticipating this party with optimistic hope that he may find a new countess, a woman who would be a mother to his daughters. Goodness, but they were in need of a feminine hand. His mother provided guidance as she could when she was at the dower house. However, she also kept a house in Bath and was spending increasingly more time there. So much, in fact, that Roth wondered if she might have a gentleman friend.

If he was intent on remarrying, why was he hesitating? Particularly after meeting Mrs. Dunthorpe that afternoon. His reaction to her had been swift and deep. She was indeed attractive, with her lush auburn hair and dark chocolate-colored eyes that tilted up at the edges, giving her the appearance that she was often and easily amused. He'd been instantly drawn to that idea, and then she'd been charming and witty into the bargain.

Then he'd kissed her hand. An astounding desire had overwhelmed him, an almost primal need to claim her and make her his. He hadn't felt that in… well, he'd *never* felt quite that.

And that was terrifying.

He *had* experienced an immediate attraction to his wife. Pamela had captivated him in a way that no one had in his then-twenty-six years. He'd offered for her within a week, and they were wed four weeks after that.

She'd been mostly quiet, biddable even, but he'd seen her laugh with abandon and looked forward to a future where they did that together. Only they never had. Instead, she'd grown more distant over time. Then, she'd become ill, and just before she'd died, she'd admitted a horrible truth: that marrying him had devastated her, for she'd been in love with someone else. That someone, however, had not been an earl, and her parents had insisted she wed Roth.

He sometimes wished she'd never told him. But, it explained the coldness of their marriage and her disinterest. She had, at least, adored their daughters.

"Coming, Roth?" their host, Lord Cosgrove, asked as he walked abreast of Roth on his way into the drawing room.

"Yes." Roth took a deep breath and crossed the threshold. Though he told himself to find anyone other than Mrs. Dunthorpe, he located her without effort. She stood near the hearth, a glass of wine in her hand, a stunning blue gown draping her curves. The garment boasted a minimal amount of lace and ruffles, which Roth preferred. She looked elegant and beautiful, exactly the sort of woman he would want to pursue.

But should not.

His goal in finding a wife was not to fall in love or even hold a great attraction. He'd had both of those things with Pamela, and she'd broken his heart—cleanly and irrevocably. Not only did he not wish to love again, he wasn't sure he could.

What he *was* certain of was that he wanted a mother for his daughters and perhaps the opportunity to produce an heir. Even that wasn't entirely necessary. He had a younger brother who would be more than capable of succeeding him, and, unlike Roth, he already had a son.

No, on the whole, Mrs. Dunthorpe was a risk he didn't need to take. He would do best to ignore the extraordinary pull he felt toward her and direct his attentions elsewhere.

Except, he'd asked her to save a dance for him. He was beholden to that at least. Best to get it over with, then.

Roth made his way toward her. Just before he reached her, she looked toward him. Their gazes met and locked, and again, he had a primitive desire to toss her over his shoulder and carry her upstairs. Then everyone would know that she belonged to him.

This was a disaster.

He smiled widely and bowed. "Good evening, Mrs. Dunthorpe." They'd been seated at opposite ends of the table for dinner, so he hadn't spoken to her since that afternoon.

She dipped into a shallow curtsey. Honestly, their formality was unnecessary and even a trifle laughable given their location at an intimate house party. Why were they doing it?

He supposed he was trying to keep things formal and above reproach. As if that would dam the torrent of longing cascading through him.

"Good evening, Roth," she said, her warm, seductive tone stoking his arousal. "You gentlemen did not linger long over your port."

He leaned close, and his nostrils filled with lily of the valley. He tried not to think of how delightful she would smell if he pressed his lips and nose to her bare flesh. "Lord Cosgrove suggested we join the ladies sooner rather than later."

"I see. I suppose the reasoning behind this party would suggest the goal is for us to mingle." She sipped her wine, her alluring eyes still meeting his over the rim of her glass.

Was she flirting with him? Or at least alluding to the matching part of the party? Had she come here to remarry or for another more temporary purpose? When he'd asked her if she no longer wished to be alone, she'd been evasive.

The idea of a liaison with her filled his mind. He might welcome a short, torrid affair. There would be no risk of a romantic attachment, of hearts being lost or broken.

He was getting ahead of himself. Hadn't he planned to dance with her and be done with the matter? And then what—ignore her for the duration of the party? Roth couldn't see that happening. Their numbers weren't even thirty. Avoiding her would be impossible at best and noticeably rude at worst.

"The dancing is about to begin," Roth said. "I've come to claim our dance."

She smiled, her brows arching briefly. "Oh, splendid. Do forgive me if I misstep. It's been a long time since I've danced." She finished her wine and set her empty glass on a nearby table.

Roth considered offering her his arm, but they didn't have far to walk.

Lord and Lady Cosgrove stood in the middle of the makeshift dancefloor. Half the room had been cleared of furniture and a pianoforte stood in the corner.

"The dancing will begin imminently with Lady Cosgrove calling," Lord Cosgrove announced, then sent a loving smile toward his wife. "Please welcome Mr. Henry Goodlands, a most accomplished musician who will be with us this week."

A gentleman in his middle-forties moved toward the pianoforte and bowed. He took his seat.

Roth watched their host guide their hostess into place. He'd known them a long time, and their love was as palpable as their good nature. Their marriage was enviable, and for a time after Pamela's death, Roth had distanced himself from the Cosgroves and others like them. Seeing others so deeply and mutually in love was a pain he hadn't been able to bear.

"Shall we take our places?" Mrs. Dunthorpe asked, interrupting his reverie.

"Of course." Roth guided her to the longways formation.

"Let us stand at the end so I can watch and reacquaint myself," she said softly.

"Certainly." They took their places at each end of the line. Roth watched her as she focused intently on the dance, her eyes following Lord and Lady Cosgrove as they stepped to the music.

Once the next couple began to lead, Mrs. Dunthorpe seemed to relax, her features smoothing.

"It's all come back to you now?" he asked across the space that separated them.

"I believe so. We'll find out shortly." She gave him a saucy look that made his gut clench with longing.

As it happened, she acquitted herself beautifully. She was light and sure of step, and her laughter only increased Roth's enjoyment. When the dance finished, her cheeks held a pretty pink flush.

"Would you care for something to drink after our exertions?"

"Yes, please."

This time, he offered his arm. Not because the refreshments were so far away, but because he simply couldn't allow another opportunity for touching to pass.

She curled her hand about his forearm, closer to the elbow than the wrist. Roth resisted the urge to put his other hand over hers, to stroke her bare fingers. No one had donned gloves this evening.

"Why has it been so long since you've danced?" Roth asked.

"Birmingham's social opportunities are not as robust as those in London, I imagine. Our season will begin soon and last through the winter."

"But there are balls and assemblies, surely."

She shot him a slightly teasing look. "Yes, but I am somewhat of a widow wallflower. Gentlemen much prefer to partner with young, unwed ladies."

That was nearly a crime, for Mrs. Dunthorpe was every bit as comely and captivating as any young, unwed lady. He guessed her to be close to thirty, and if she'd been alone for a decade, which she'd indicated, she would have been a young widowed lady in possession of a great deal of charm and beauty. Roth found it odd that she would not have been partnered. Or remarried.

Perhaps she didn't want to be, you dolt.

Perhaps she even still mourned her husband.

They encountered a footman with a tray of drinks. "What would you like?" Roth asked her.

"There is hock, sherry, and port," the footman offered.

"Hock, please."

Roth plucked up a glass of the pale wine and handed it to her. Then he grabbed a glass of port for himself.

She took her hand from his arm, and he contented himself with the fact that they stood close to one another. He tapped his glass gently to hers. "To new acquaintances."

"And to dancing," she added with a sparkle in her eye.

After swallowing his sip of port, Roth grasped for one of the dozens of questions he wanted to ask her. "Do you hail from Birmingham, then?"

"I moved there after I wed. And where is your estate?"

"My family seat, Ludlow Court, is in southern Yorkshire, but I spend a great deal of my time in London and elsewhere."

"I shouldn't have assumed you have just one estate," she said with a laugh. "Perhaps you have a dozen."

"I have two. And a hunting lodge near Lancaster. Indeed, I and some of the gentlemen from the party, along with some others, will be traveling there after the party concludes. I confess I am less of a sporting fellow than I am someone who simply enjoys the outdoors. I have many fond memories of Lune Lodge with my father and grandfather."

"That sounds lovely. Do you ever take your daughters there?"

He stared at her. "To a hunting lodge?"

Mrs. Dunthorpe laughed. "You appear shocked. You said you go primarily to enjoy being outside. I thought your daughters might also appreciate that."

"They did. Rather, Violet did. She has reached the ripe age of nine and has declared that she can no longer allow herself to become dirty. Rosamund, on the other hand, is delighted to march all over the countryside. She even likes to fish." He chuckled. "She may be more of a sportsman than I am."

Grinning, Mrs. Dunthorpe asked. "And how old is she?"

"Six."

"She sounds delightful, and perhaps is occasionally a handful?"

"They both can be, which is why I should like for them to have a mother. My mother lives in the dowager house at Ludlow Court, but she also has a residence in Bath. The girls come with me to London for the Season. I don't like to be away from them that long."

Mrs. Dunthorpe's sable eyes softened. "You sound like a doting father. Mine was like that. I miss him every day."

"I'm sorry he's no longer with you," Roth said softly. "What of your mother?"

"She died when I was young. I don't remember her at all. It was always just me and my father."

She *had* been alone.

"Along with the others who worked at the inn." Her cheeks flushed again, and she hurriedly took a long sip of wine.

Did she regret saying that? Roth was too curious to let the comment pass without inquiry. He wanted to know absolutely everything about her. "What inn?"

"My father owned an inn. That is where I grew up. The people there—the cook, the maids, the groomsmen—they were my family."

Her father had owned an inn. She seemed as

though she came from different stock in that she didn't possess the haughtiness or social superiority that was inherent in many of his class. He suddenly felt like a judgmental ass.

"I imagine that sounds rather foreign to you." Her smile was engaging and warm—not at all judgmental. She'd seen right through him and hadn't stalked away in disgust. It seemed impossible he could like her more, but he did.

"It sounds different. It also sounds lovely, as if you had a close-knit group of people who cared for you and about for whom you cared."

"They were very dear to me. Though my father is gone, most of them still work at the inn. He had to sell it when he became ill."

Roth heard the tinge of sorrow in her voice, but before he could offer comfort, she brightened and continued speaking. "Enough of that. Tell me about London. I have never been."

"It's busy and beautiful, but also crowded and dirty in places. I like the parks and the theatre. I particularly enjoy taking a drive to Richmond."

"What of the Season and Parliament? I imagine that is a whirlwind."

"It can be," he said. "I've avoided the social events of the Season for the past five years, since my wife passed away. I've preferred to focus my energy on my obligations in the Lords."

"I can understand wanting to do that," she said with a soft understanding. "What are your obligations?"

"I chair a few committees. I am especially dedicated to the places I mentioned before. Many are in disrepair in addition to being crowded and filthy. Everyone deserves safe housing."

"Indeed they do." She sounded impressed. "What

an admirable position for you to take. I hope your peers listen to you."

He let out a short, sharp laugh. "Not as often as I would like, but I won't stop trying to persuade them."

"I can see why you wouldn't have time for the activities of the Season with your work and your daughters. What do they like to do in London?"

"Violet has declared that she wants to visit Bond Street this year." He shook his head. "She'll be ten by then and insists it's necessary for her to learn to shop, especially since she doesn't have a mother." He gave her a wry look. "Do you see why I must find a wife?"

Mrs. Dunthorpe laughed. "It's clearly a desperate situation. I will hope you find a new countess by the new year."

"Thank you. I appreciate the support." He studied her a moment, unable to discern if she might be interested in that. There was no indication that she was.

There was also no indication that she *wasn't*.

One of the younger fellows in attendance, Mr. Jacob Emerson, came toward them. Roth suspected his time with Mrs. Dunthorpe was about to come to an end. At least for tonight.

"I think I'm about to lose you," he murmured.

She arched her brow in question but wasn't able to ask anything—if she'd wanted to—because Emerson arrived. He glanced toward Roth and inclined his head before turning his full attention to Mrs. Dunthorpe.

"I couldn't help but take notice of your grace on the dance floor, Mrs. Dunthorpe. I hoped you might allow me to partner you in the next dance." Emerson's expression was earnest if slightly nervous. He appeared to be the youngest gentleman in attendance. Roth estimated he was twenty-five. Surely Mrs. Dunthorpe needed a man of more...maturity.

Roth reminded himself that Emerson was asking her to dance, not proposing marriage. He also reminded himself that he was putting the proverbial cart before the horse.

The truth struck him like a slap to the face: he was jealous. Though he'd just met Mrs. Dunthorpe that very afternoon, he wanted to have her entirely to himself.

"I would be most obliged, Mr. Emerson," she said. Then she turned her head to Roth and gave him a dazzling smile that soothed his baser emotions. "Thank you for the delightful conversation."

"Thank *you*." He took her hand and lightly pressed his lips to her knuckles. Though he longed to linger there, he released her. "I look forward to our next encounter."

And he prayed it would not be too long in coming.

CHAPTER 3

$\mathcal{T}$he final performance of the talent display the following afternoon, Lord Cosgrove strumming a guitar, finished to a rousing round of applause. Lady Cosgrove had recruited her guests to share a skill, and those who'd dared to participate had taken their turn atop the dais in the ballroom. Charlotte had declined to perform, as she'd had no idea what to do.

The talents had ranged from reciting Shakespeare or poetry to singing to Mr. Emerson attempting—and rather failing—to juggle apples. Charlotte noted that Roth hadn't taken part either. He'd sat in the row behind her, not close enough to exchange pleasantries, unfortunately.

Hopefully, they would have a chance to speak now that the show had concluded. She kept thinking of their conversation last night. His love for his daughters and interest in helping the poor were particularly endearing. He was not only ridiculously handsome and charming; he possessed integrity and an irresistible love for his family.

He'd also seemed slightly perturbed by Emerson's interruption. The earl's eyes had narrowed for a fleeting moment. Perhaps Charlotte had imagined it. Or, perhaps she'd correctly ascertained Roth's instant passion for her. *Or*, most likely, she'd completely fabricated his reaction so that she would not feel silly in nursing her own sudden and inexplicable yearning for him.

Now, in the light of the following day, she realized how nonsensical all that was. At thirty, she was simply coming to terms with being alone and the near certainty that she always would be.

"There are refreshments at the back of the ballroom," Lady Cosgrove announced.

Eager to speak with Roth, Charlotte stood. However, before she could make her way toward the earl, Emerson, who'd also risen, turned to her. "Did I embarrass myself horribly with the juggling?"

"Not at all," she assured him. "You were most diverting."

"I was able to juggle years ago at Cambridge. I suppose I should have practiced last night." He chuckled. "Would you care for a glass of wine or ratafia?" He inclined his head toward where the refreshments were spread across a table. A footman stood sentinel at each end.

Charlotte moved her gaze toward where Roth had been sitting, but he wasn't there. She scanned the room and saw him standing away from the seating area. He was turning away and began walking to the door.

No, he couldn't leave!

Nor was she going to run after him and provoke raised eyebrows or worse, gossip. "A glass of ratafia would not come amiss," she said with a forced smile.

She took Emerson's arm as he guided her to the refreshment table. The footman served their drinks, and Charlotte spent the next quarter hour listening to Emerson regale her with how he started juggling and his intent to hone his skill once more. As soon as they were joined by other guests, she excused herself and made her way sedately from the ballroom.

Where had Roth gone? She'd seen other gentlemen leave and assumed they'd gone to the billiards room. That seemed to be where the men congregated.

Consequently, she saw no point in going there. Accepting defeat, she went to the Landscape Room, a small chamber located near the library where there were purportedly several landscape paintings, including one by Charlotte's favorite painter, Richard Wilson.

Favorite? In truth, he was the one famous landscape painter whose work she'd seen. An older lady in Birmingham with whom she was friends owned one of his paintings, a ruined castle next to a lake. Charlotte found it provocative and even a little haunting. She was curious to see what this one was like and if it would evoke the same sensations.

Charlotte stepped into the Landscape Room and abruptly stopped. Standing at the opposite side, surveying a painting, was Roth. At least, she was fairly certain it was the earl. She hadn't committed his appearance from the rear to memory. The hair was definitely the same wheaten color, and the breadth of his shoulders and tapered waist supported his identity.

Perhaps it was wrong of her to stand there and stare at him, but she found she couldn't speak. She'd hoped to see him. Longed to spend more time with him. And here he was. Alone.

He moved from the back wall to the right side, his attention shifting to the next painting on display. His head turned slightly toward her, then snapped fully in her direction. "Mrs. Dunthorpe?"

"I came to view the Wilson."

"It's lovely. Come see." He gestured for her to join him as he pivoted and walked to the center of the opposite wall. "Are you an admirer of Wilson?"

"I, ah, like the one I've seen." She slid him a slightly disconcerted look. He was so worldly, particularly when compared with her.

"I do appreciate his landscapes. I especially like the light in this one."

Charlotte looked at the painting and tried to ignore the gentleman standing beside her. Except, there was no hope of that. What she needed to do was ignore the way his proximity made her feel. Warm and heavy. Anxious.

Breathless.

Blinking, she took a stuttered breath and perused the landscape. The sun was setting on the right of the canvas, casting a warm glow over the rest of the painting, which Charlotte imagined she could feel. No, that was the heat of Roth's arm grazing hers.

"The sky looks incredibly real." There were wispy clouds amidst the pale blue and gold. A river meandered through the center, reflecting the dusky light.

"It reminds me of a warm summer evening when I was young," Roth said softly. "My father took me and my younger brother to the River Don. Papa taught us how to skip rocks. Then we stripped down to just our breeches—even Papa—and splashed about until it was nearly dark."

Charlotte smiled as she turned her head toward him. "How old were you?"

Roth also turned his head, and their faces were so very close. "Eight. My brother, Simon, was six."

"Sounds like a wonderful memory. I've a similar one with my father, but it was a brook, not a river. We went every Sunday after church. Well, on the

Sundays that he attended. He wasn't able to go every week, but he made sure I was there." She lowered her voice to a conspiratorial whisper. "I rather had to since the vicar gave me lessons on everything from geography to history to rudimentary Latin."

Roth's eyes widened slightly. "You speak Latin?"

"Goodness, no. I can read it—passably. I did manage to speak some French, but I'm out of practice. Once in a while, I converse with a friend." The lady who owned the Wilson landscape, in fact.

"You astonish me, Mrs. Dunthorpe." He spoke in a satiny tone, shimmering with admiration.

Charlotte jerked her focus back to the painting lest she become completely lost in the fathomless depths of Roth's glittering green eyes. "You came to see the Wilson too?"

"Actually, I came to see a landscape by Cosgrove's cousin. He said it was mediocre, but he'd felt beholden to display it somewhere. Then he sniggered and said the painting was most...*conversational.* I took that to mean there was something unique about it."

"And is there?"

"I haven't found it yet. Cosgrove said it centered on a folly at his father's estate—he's the Duke of Ironbridge. In any case, I've only encountered one painting with a folly and it was off in the background, so I don't think that's it. Besides, it was also better than mediocre, at least in my opinion, although there wasn't anything particularly *conversational* about it."

"That's the beauty of art, though," Charlotte said, glancing about the room at the two dozen or so landscapes adorning the space. "What is mediocre to Lord Cosgrove may be exemplary to you."

"And utter rubbish to you." Roth laughed. "I jest.

Somehow, I think you would find something to praise about anything or anyone."

"Why is that?"

He shrugged. "I suppose you seem particularly kindhearted. Generous. Or perhaps I'm merely smitten by your charm." He fluttered his lashes at her as if he were a coquette.

Charlotte snorted and immediately wished she could take it back. Her hand flew to her face, as if she could push the sound back in. "Pardon me," she murmured.

Grinning, Roth shook his head. "I will not. That snort was also charming."

"That's kind of you to say, but it's not something I typically do around...others." She'd been about to say attractive gentlemen, but decided they were already too close and their conversation too intimate.

Intimate?

Because she felt comfortable with him. At ease enough to snort, apparently.

"We are looking for a landscape with a prominently placed folly, then?" she asked, thinking it best to divert the conversation from themselves.

He arched a blond brow. "Are we? I should appreciate the company. It doesn't appear to be on this wall or the back, and I was just in the middle of surveying that one." He gestured across the room where he'd pivoted after she'd surreptitiously watched him.

Spied on him was perhaps a better description.

No, she wasn't spying. She'd been...appreciating. As if he were a painting.

Charlotte grimaced inwardly.

"You're welcome to review the walls I already looked over. In fact, you should, as there are several lovely landscapes."

"I think I'm committed to finding the conversational folly, but once we've located it, I may take a turn about the room."

"Very well. Shall we continue?" He turned, and she followed him to the other wall.

"You left the talent show rather quickly," Charlotte said, going right back to discussing what she'd just abandoned: them. More specifically, *him*.

They'd stopped in front of a landscape with horses grazing in a wide field, a large oak standing sentinel to one side. She looked over at Roth's profile, which showed the strong jut of his chin and the impossibly long curl of his eyelashes. "Was it not to your liking?"

"I will say that it was diverting—some of the performances more than others."

"Why didn't you perform?"

He sent her a coy glance. "Why didn't *you*?"

"I don't like being the center of attention in a large group. It was hard enough when I had to share something during last night's introductions." At Cecilia's instruction, they'd gathered in a large circle and taken turns telling everyone something about themselves. She'd said that she liked the quiet of late night and early morning.

As soon as the words had left her mouth, she'd realized that saying so could have been interpreted as a subtle invitation to seek her company at those hours. If it had been a regular house party, she wouldn't have thought so, but this was a matchmaking party to join people as spouses or lovers. Thankfully, no one had come to her door in the middle of the night.

Regrettably, that meant Roth hadn't either.

"I'm confident you would have acquitted yourself most admirably. You couldn't have done worse than Emerson with his juggling." He smiled. "I do believe he was trying to be amusing."

"I believe so. He hadn't practiced and thought he would have better recalled the skill from his days at Cambridge. He told me that's where he learned. Lacking skill, why not strive for laughter instead?"

"He certainly accomplished that." Roth pivoted slightly toward her. "Is that what you and he were discussing after the performances?"

He'd seen her speaking with Emerson? And did his tone venture a bit further than simple curiosity?

"Yes," she replied. "He told me all about his juggling experience. He plans to hone his skill once more."

"Then he'll be prepared for the next time he's called upon to display a talent. That is why I didn't participate. I had nothing to demonstrate." He cocked his head. "Clearly, this is not the painting we are looking for." He moved to the next one, and she joined him in front of the landscape featuring a waterfall.

"I do like this one," she said. The water in the painting seemed to move, as if it were truly cascading. "You could have danced. You're quite good at that."

He turned toward her, chuckling. "And how would I have done that by myself? Unless... you could have partnered me. Then we both would have participated."

She faced him, enjoying herself more than she had in ages. "And what dance would we have demonstrated with just the two of us?"

His nose wrinkled and his forehead creased as he considered her question. Finally, he suggested, "The minuet?"

"I don't know the steps, so perhaps not."

"I could have taught you. Or, there is a dance in Austria that's quite popular. It's called the waltz and is danced by two people. There is touching and a rather close proximity for the entirety of the dance." His gaze, entangled with hers, was unwavering. "Very scandalous."

The air around them heated, and Charlotte fought not to take a step toward him. They were only two paces apart. She could be in his arms in less than a breath...

"Do you know how it goes?"

"Not specifically." His brows leapt and his eyes gleamed. "I know—we could have created our own dance. I fear we've missed an opportunity here, Mrs. Dunthorpe."

How she longed for him to call her Charlotte! "Have we? I see an empty room with a paucity of furniture. Surely, we could come up with our dance here."

"To what end?" he asked with a slight but very mischievous grin.

She lifted a shoulder. "Do we need a reason? On occasion, I find it's pleasant to do something simply because it sounds...fun."

"I can't argue with that. How should our dance look? Should it be triple time? Double?"

Charlotte put a hand to her cheek. "You've quite lost me now. I've no idea."

"Perhaps we should start with the minuet and adapt our dance from there."

"I've told you, I don't know how."

"Then it's good that my grandmother taught me, and I can now teach you. It's six steps forward and six back. Watch my feet." He moved farther away from the wall and demonstrated the steps.

"They're somewhat halting."

"That's a good way to describe it." He clasped her hand, surprising her. She didn't quite gasp, but she inhaled swiftly. His gaze shot briefly to hers. He'd heard it. His thumb moved gently over her fingers. "Ready to try?"

"No, but we're making this up, aren't we? I don't like halting steps. I would rather do something more animated."

He released her hand, and she kept herself from frowning. "Show me."

Charlotte made little skipping steps and added a hop, then a turn. "More like that."

Now Roth snorted. "My apologies, but that looks far too athletic. I thought we were aiming for something more sedate, more...intimate."

She met his gaze with a taunting stare. "Sedate sounds boring."

"Mmm, it does." He looked at her intently. "And intimate? How does that sound?"

A delightful shiver raced across her shoulders. "Scandalous, like your waltz."

"It isn't *my* waltz." He tapped his finger against his jaw. "I believe there is twirling."

"You also mentioned touching. Should we hold hands again?"

He nodded in faux solemnity. "I think we must if we're to do our dance justice."

She held out her hand, and he took it, his fingers warm against hers. "If we're to be scandalous, I feel as though I should touch you with my other hand as well."

He quickly clasped that appendage. "Yes, I believe this feels right. Shall we twirl?"

Moving them in a slow circle, she clasped his hands more tightly. "It can be just this? Surely we ought to progress somewhere?"

"We can twirl as if we are in a line such as in a longways formation?" He guided her to the other end of the room, but as they started back, she lost her balance and had to grip him more tightly.

She giggled. "I'm quite dizzy. Too much twirling."

"I must agree. I feel as though I've drunk too much port."

"Oh, I did that once. It was dreadful. I thought the entire house was spinning around me."

He looked into her eyes. "I hope this isn't dreadful."

"Far from it," she said softly. "I do think the dance would benefit from being closer together. That way, if the twirling makes one dizzy, they are in close proximity to their partner, who may rescue them from certain doom."

He pulled her closer, his hands moving up to her elbows. "You make an excellent point. Shall we try again, with gentler turns?"

She put her palms against his chest. "I think I need to hold on to you somehow."

"Clasp my shoulders, then. Or my neck even."

Charlotte held her breath as she slid her hands up to his shoulders. His hands moved from her elbows to her waist.

"Holding on to your arms seemed incredibly awkward," he nearly whispered. "Is this acceptable?"

More than. If only he would pull her fully against him. And then lower his lips to hers...

"Shall we dance?" she asked, sounding as breathless as she felt. Was she even breathing at all?

He moved her in a slow, gentle circle, his eyes never leaving hers. "I would hum a tune, but I've no idea what. I'm afraid you'll have to imagine something."

She was imagining plenty, and none of it had a thing to do with music. Her hands inched closer toward his neck as they twirled. There was no dizziness this time, just a persistent, delicious heat swirling in her belly.

When they'd returned to where they started, he brought them to a halt. "That was lovely. What shall we call it?"

"The Landscape Twirl?"

"Brilliant." He stared into her eyes a moment longer. Would he kiss her?

Then his gaze shifted to a point behind her, his lips parting. "There it is!"

Reluctantly, Charlotte took her hands from his shoulders and turned her head. She instantly saw what he meant—a painting with a folly at its center. It was on the wall behind the door. "I see that Lord Cosgrove hung that in the least prominent place in the room."

Roth chuckled. "So it would seem. Come, we must see what the fuss is." He released her waist, but slid one hand to her lower back, keeping his palm against her as they walked to the painting.

The folly sat atop a hill and was an open-air temple with columns. Inside the temple, a woman sat on a bench with her skirts slightly raised. Between her legs was the unmistakable lower half of a man, his upper half hidden beneath her garments.

Now, Charlotte did gasp. "Is he...?"

"Pleasuring her? It would appear that he is...ah, yes."

Charlotte tore her gaze from the painting to look at Roth. His attention was not on the painting, but on her. He regarded her with slitted eyes, his teasing nature gone in favor of an unmistakable smoldering desire.

"Well, that is certainly bound to spark a conversation," Charlotte murmured as need pulsed through her.

"Or something else. Something far more...primal." He moved closer so that only a breath separated them.

"Yes," she hissed softly, desperate for him to kiss her. If he did not, she was simply going to have to give in to her wanton impulses and commence ravishing *him*.

CHAPTER 4

The urge to kiss Mrs. Dunthorpe nearly overwhelmed him. But surely he shouldn't be kissing someone he referred to as "Mrs. Dunthorpe." Nevertheless, he longed to do so.

He hadn't experienced this depth of longing in a very long time. It was almost terrifying. No, it was actually definitely terrifying. He didn't want to feel this strong of a pull toward anyone.

And yet, he did. He wanted nothing more than to wrap her in his arms and kiss her until they both forgot what they were even doing in the Landscape Room.

The *Landscape Room*. He couldn't kiss her here.

Did that mean he would consider doing so someplace else? Such as her bedchamber or his? Was he contemplating a liaison?

Slow down.

Taking things too quickly had led him to romantic disappointment. He would not make the same mistake twice.

He nearly turned back toward the painting, but decided that would be a very bad idea given the *conversational* nature of it. Instead, he pivoted to the middle of the room and took a step away from her to cool his ardor. "Why is it you've come to Blickton for the house party?" He suddenly needed to know her intentions and whether they matched his.

She didn't immediately respond, and he faced her once more. Her features were unreadable, not as they'd been a few moments earlier when they'd nearly kissed. "Mostly to see my friend, Lady Cosgrove," she finally said.

"Mostly?" he asked, hating that he might have disappointed her by not kissing her. But he was trying to behave like a gentleman, even if his thoughts since making her acquaintance had been distinctly ungentlemanly.

"Why did you come?" she asked.

"To perchance make a match. To remarry," he clarified. As he had last night, he imagined something entirely different with her—a temporary, passionate affair that would satisfy this blistering attraction he felt for her.

He ought to run far away. He could not—would not—lose his heart a second time. He wasn't even sure he still had one, not a romantic heart anyway. All the love he had, he gave to his daughters, and that was as it should be.

She smiled at him, softly at first and then more brilliantly, with genuine warmth. "Yes, to find a mother for your daughters, I believe. I wish you the best of luck in your search. Please excuse me, I do think I require a respite before dinner."

As she walked toward the door, he took a step, intending to stop her. To what end? He wouldn't need to run away if she departed. This was for the best.

After she was gone, he realized he was holding his breath. He let it out in a soft whoosh. Then he swore.

With a final glare toward the lewd painting, he

stalked from the Landscape Room and made his way upstairs to his chamber. He could do with a respite too.

Or a cold bath.

Or a frigging.

Or both.

Roth walked straight through his bedchamber to the dressing room. His valet, Dyer, was polishing Roth's Hessians and looked up.

"My lord, is aught amiss?"

"No." Roth started to take off his coat, but Dyer set the boot aside and leapt up to give assistance. "I'd like a bath."

"Of course." Dyer carefully set the coat on Roth's trunk.

Roth loosened his cravat. "I'll have a glass of brandy while you ready the bath."

"I recognize that furrowed brow," Dyer said. "What is troubling you?" He took the cravat from Roth and set it atop the coat.

"You know me too well."

Dyer, perhaps the most elegant man Roth had ever known, arched his dark brow. "I have been your valet for nearly twenty years. I should hope so."

He'd also been a valued confidante. No one had truly understood the depth of Roth's devastation after learning his wife had only married him for his title, that the love he'd felt for her had been entirely one-sided. Because Roth hadn't told anyone else the truth.

"I've met a woman at the party."

"I believe that was the point," Dyer said wryly. "Let me pour your brandy." He went into the bedchamber, and Roth followed him.

When the valet handed him the glass, Roth took a

sip and welcomed the heat of the spirt as it slid down his throat. "This woman is unlike any other I've met."

"*Any* other?"

"The...strength of my reaction to her reminds me somewhat of Pamela."

There was understanding and sympathy in Dyer' astute blue gaze. "I see. I imagine that concerns you."

"It bloody terrifies me. I won't suffer that again." Roth took a longer drink of brandy and moved to the hearth, where a low fire burned.

"It is improbable that you would wed someone else like her ladyship."

Roth shot a look toward the valet. "It is still possible, however. Plenty of people wed to align themselves or their family with nobility or someone higher in the peerage." That had been Pamela's family's goal—for her, as the granddaughter of a baron, to marry as far above her station as possible.

"I can't see you wedding someone who was interested in anything other than a deep, abiding love."

Roth thought he'd done that the first time. Pamela had told him she loved him, that he was her dream come true. He'd believed every word. "I'd prefer to enter into my second marriage with the appropriate expectations." Which was to say: none. Could he even expect loyalty? At least Pamela had been faithful. As far as he knew.

"That is most cynical. That goes against your very nature," Dyer said quietly.

"I have to be cynical about this." Roth knew he sounded cold, but what could he do? He'd been fooled once, and he would not allow that to happen again. "Pamela lied to me for the duration of our marriage. Only guilt prompted her to reveal the truth before she died. And I can't even be sure she told me everything. For all I know, she carried on with the man she loved while we were wed."

"I wish you wouldn't torture yourself. You've no evidence she was ever unfaithful."

No, he did not, but Roth had felt so utterly betrayed by her. It was difficult not to think that even when she'd unburdened herself, she hadn't been completely truthful. Why would he trust her after learning their entire marriage had been a lie?

At least he could be certain of his daughters' parentage. They both carried physical traits that were decidedly Ludlow. Violet's nose and chin were most definitely his, and Rosamund's eyes were a mirror of his own.

"I would caution you against disallowing yourself the opportunity to fall in love with someone who will reciprocate your sentiments. I think it's far more likely *that* will happen than what you've already endured."

Roth took another sip of brandy and sent Dyer a faint smirk. "You are too optimistic for your own good."

"Optimism has always served me well, particularly when I accepted a position as valet to a seventeen-year-old boy who instead wished to promote a young footman because he gave him advice on how to pleasure a lady."

Roth pressed his lips together. It had been some time since Dyer had brought up *that* matter. When Roth's father had insisted on hiring Dyer and not the young footman, Roth had pouted for a week. "Those are useful skills for a valet, particularly when he is attending a young man."

"Certainly, but a valet ought to also know how to style hair and assemble a smart ensemble."

"I am not going to argue that you were not the

better choice." Rother gave him a suffering look. "Did you have a point?"

"That if I were not optimistic, I might have accepted the other offer I received—to be valet to the Duke of Evesham."

Roth blinked. "You never told me that."

Dyer shrugged. "Nevertheless, it is true."

"Why would you turn down Evesham?" Roth shook his head with a chuckle. "Actually, *how* could you turn him down? I'd be afraid he'd ruin me if I got on his bad side."

"I made sure there was another candidate who would be a better fit for His Grace. In any case, I took my chance on you, and I have not regretted it for a moment." His dark brows pitched low. "However, if you continue along this path of isolating yourself from the possibility of romantic happiness, I may change my mind."

Roth knew the man meant well, but he was taking his meddling too far. "How is it a man who has never wed feels confident in counseling me on such matters?"

"I have regrets," Dyer responded softly, surprising Roth. "They just aren't to do with you. I would hate for you to look back twenty years on and wish you'd made a different choice."

Setting his brandy on the mantel, Roth took a step toward the valet. "I hope you didn't choose me over love." Roth wasn't sure he could bear it.

"No, I did not. It was…before. And it no longer signifies, except to be a cautionary tale for you. Pardon me, for I must attend to your bath."

Roth watched the man, whom he admired very much, retreat to the dressing room. From there, he'd access the servants' corridor and make his way downstairs to arrange the bath.

What—or whom—had Dyer not chosen? Did the decision haunt him, or was it a distant memory that only vaguely pulled at his heart now and again?

How Roth hoped that day would come for his feelings regarding Pamela. It was not yet a long-ago sadness that he could recall without a sense of loss or enmity. Someday…

Until then, he couldn't afford to be optimistic.

What Dyer *had* clarified for him, however, was that Roth ought not to be thinking of his baser needs. He was no longer a lad desperate for romantic and sexual interaction. He was an earl and a father.

Picking up his glass, he tossed back the rest of the brandy. He needed a mother for his girls, not a woman with the potential to make him feel things he was much better off not feeling.

~

*C*harlotte half listened to the conversation amongst some of the ladies in the drawing room. She couldn't seem to keep herself from watching the door to see if Roth would arrive.

She'd barely spoken two words to him since their encounter in the Landscape Room the previous afternoon. They'd said "good evening" last night before dinner and nothing more. Cecilia had seated Charlotte next to Lord Audlington. He'd been a charming and attentive conversationalist. She'd cast surreptitious glances toward Roth, but, as far as she could tell, he hadn't looked at her even once.

It seemed he was uncomfortable in her presence now. Perhaps he'd found her too forward yesterday when she'd practically thrown herself into him as she'd anticipated his kiss.

She'd been so sure he was about to put his lips to

hers that when he did not, she had to stop herself from reacting. To keep from frowning, she'd pressed her lips together. Then she'd curled her hands into fists lest she grab him by the lapels and kiss him until they were both witless.

Mrs. Fitzwarren occupied the space to Charlotte's right on the settee. A widow, but then they were all widows—or, in Charlotte's case, purported to be—she was a few years older than Charlotte, with four children. Her gray eyes sparkled with a hint of mischief as she leaned slightly forward. "I thought we could share why we're all here."

"I should think that would be obvious," Mrs. Wynne-Hargest, a Welshwoman, said with a laugh.

"Is anyone interested in remarriage?" Mrs. Fitzwarren grimaced. "I confess it's difficult to contemplate after five years of independence following ten years of childbearing. I'm still young enough to conceive again, and I just don't think I want to endure that even once more."

Charlotte noted that several other women nodded in agreement. Based on that, it was easy to see which ones were mothers—Mrs. Fitzwarren, Mrs. Wynne-Hargest, Mrs. Grey, and Lady Clinton. In their circle of six ladies, only Mrs. Sheldon was childless like Charlotte. They exchanged a quick, commiserative glance, though Charlotte had no way of knowing how Mrs. Sheldon felt about not being a mother. For Charlotte, it was an ache she'd grown accustomed to. It was simply something she must endure.

"I'd have more children," Mrs. Wynne-Hargest said with a smile. "I enjoyed carrying, and babies are so lovely. Motherhood is, in many ways, better than matrimony."

The other mothers laughed in response. Mrs.

Grey nodded vigorously. "Motherhood was the only rewarding part of matrimony, in my experience. Thank goodness for my children." Her features seemed to glow, a visible representation of the love she felt.

Charlotte resisted the urge to jump up and leave. She simply couldn't contribute to this part of the conversation and listening to it made her surprisingly sad.

Lady Clinton looked to Mrs. Fitzwarren. "So, no remarriage for you?"

"I might consider it in the right circumstances. And before you ask what those are, I don't know." Mrs. Fitzwarren laughed and was joined by several others. She turned her head toward Charlotte. "What about you, Mrs. Dunthorpe? Would you take another husband?"

She would have been delighted to have taken one at all, let alone a second. Alas, she'd been robbed of that chance and done the best she could with the consequences.

Just as she was about to answer Mrs. Fitzwarren, Roth entered the drawing room with Mrs. Make-peace, who was perhaps the most attractive widow there. She was certainly the youngest. Just twenty-five, with dark blonde hair and alluring hazel eyes, she possessed a musical laugh and curved figure garbed in the latest style so that she looked as if she'd just walked out of a London ballroom during the height of the Season.

"I may consider it." Charlotte wanted to swallow the words back. She hadn't meant to say that, because of course she *couldn't* consider marriage, not without revealing her past, which included how she'd managed to survive as a "widow" for all these years. "We aren't sharing this information with the gentlemen, are we?" she added. "I am not on the hunt for a husband and would hate to give the wrong impression."

"Completely understandable," Mrs. Hatcliff-Lind said with a fierce nod. "This stays between us ladies."

Charlotte wanted to believe that, but knew how easy it was to let things slip. Easy for others, anyway. If there was anyone better at holding secrets than her, she hadn't met them. And that was because she had very important ones to keep.

Turning to her left, she eyed Lady Clinton, who was seated in a chair situated between the two settees that faced each other.

"I suppose it's my turn," Lady Clinton said with a sniff. "I have married for love and for security. I would eagerly do the former again, but have no interest in the latter. Unfortunately, I do not expect love to strike me twice."

Mrs. Fitzwarren sent an encouraging smile toward Lady Clinton. "You never know. My sister has been in love more than once."

Next came Mrs. Sheldon, but Charlotte didn't hear what she said because she was watching Roth with Mrs. Makepeace. They stood near the windows, talking and smiling. It seemed he preferred her company to Charlotte's.

Stifling a frown, Charlotte returned her attention to the conversation. Mrs. Wynne-Hargest was speaking. "It seems the majority of us are here for some temporary excitement." Her lips curved into a faint smirk. "Has anyone found that yet?"

Lady Clinton's hand fluttered to her chest. "*I* certainly wouldn't say."

"Surely we can share amongst ourselves," Mrs. Wynne-Hargest argued. "Can't we all agree that what happens at Blickton stays at Blickton?"

Some of the ladies nodded. Charlotte sat stock-still.

Mrs. Wynne-Hargest threw up her hands on an exhalation. "Fine. If it means anything, I have nothing to share, but I would have if I did. Indeed, I hope to find…engagement soon and will keep you apprised." She arched her brows with a wicked grin, and Charlotte nearly applauded. Men would have no trouble anticipating and discussing their exploits. Why couldn't women do the same?

In Charlotte's case, it was because she didn't have any. She couldn't even manage to obtain a kiss. And she'd really thought the desire she felt for Roth had been mutual.

She stole another glance in his direction, and her insides twisted. The thought of a liaison with him had been incredibly alluring. And the notion of something more was doubly intoxicating. She'd somehow allowed that idea to tease the edge of her mind, which was foolish because it simply could not be. For one, he was completely above her station. But most importantly, she couldn't tell him the truth.

Worst of all, there was every possibility that he was friends with Lord Manthorpe, the one man who could completely ruin her. An icy dread curled down her spine. She'd been wrongheaded to come here. If she possessed any sense of self-preservation, she would return to Birmingham at once.

What was she even doing here? She should have arranged to visit Cecilia another time. These people were here to wed, to find partners who would help with their broods of children. She shot a look toward Mrs. Sheldon and realized that wasn't entirely the case. Was Mrs. Sheldon also feeling as if she were on the outside of the gathering looking in?

Cecilia came into the drawing room and announced, "It's time for blindman's buff in the ballroom."

Everyone rose, but Charlotte did so slowly. Cecilia had told her that this version of blindman's buff would include kissing. Charlotte had already disliked seeing Roth with Mrs. Makepeace. She didn't want to chance having to watch them kiss too.

Instead of following everyone, she veered away in the direction of the staircase hall and, ultimately, her chamber. There, she would contemplate how to tell Cecilia that she'd like to return home.

CHAPTER 5

$\mathcal{T}$he afternoon sun was a welcome brightness after the gray gloom of the past few days. Most of the house party attendees were gathered outside the drawing room in preparation for a promenade to the River Swift.

Roth glanced about and noted that some pairs had formed. There was his friend Audlington and Mrs. Sheldon, of course. They'd shared an amorous embrace during a kissing version of blindman's buff yesterday, and then disappeared afterward. It seemed Mrs. Fitzwarren and Sir Godwin may have also formed an attachment after they were seen sitting close to one another following dinner last night. They'd left the drawing room within moments of each other, and today appeared even more intimate as they stood together, arms grazing one another, smiling and laughing. Roth could have imagined Mrs. Dunthorpe and himself doing the same.

Only she wasn't here. Indeed, he hadn't seen her since before blindman's buff the previous afternoon. Her absence at that activity had been particularly curious because he'd just seen her in the drawing room.

Everyone who'd been in there had made their way to the ballroom.

Except Mrs. Dunthorpe.

Then she hadn't attended dinner. He hadn't wanted to ask Cosgrove about her last night, and no announcement had been made. Perhaps she'd just been ill. However, Roth feared she'd left.

He made his way to where Lady Cosgrove stood near the doors that led outside from the drawing room, perhaps waiting for anyone else who might yet come outside.

"Roth, are you looking forward to the promenade?" she asked.

"I am, thank you. I'd hoped to speak with Mrs. Dunthorpe, but she's been absent. Has she, by chance, departed Blickton?"

Lady Cosgrove's eyes flickered with surprise. "She's still here. She wasn't feeling well yesterday, but I do hope she'll be joining us today." She did not sound at all certain.

And that was disheartening.

Their hostess gave him a cheerful smile. "Come, there will be wonderful refreshments and ale at the river." She went to join her husband, who turned toward everyone assembled.

"Are we all ready?" their host asked. "On the way, we'll stop at the new folly. It's not finished, but it's well underway. Then we'll continue to the river, where we'll have refreshments. Don't get lost, now!"

Lady Cosford took his arm, and they led the promenade toward the River Swift via the folly. With a last lingering look at the house, Roth nearly abandoned the excursion. Ultimately, he joined the group, walking somewhere in the middle of the procession. It seemed everyone was paired off except for him.

But then, they were a woman short since Mrs. Dunthorpe hadn't come.

They stopped at the folly, and Roth decided he would rather continue on his own to the river. At least it felt good to be outside. His daughters would have loved the jaunt to the river, particularly Rosamund. Violet would have found the folly interesting. She might have seen it as a large dollhouse, or at least a place where she could play make-believe.

The path widened into a grassy patch near the River Swift. Tables and chairs had been arranged—a picnic with blankets would have been a mess with the rain that had fallen the past few days—and a trio of footmen stood at the ready.

Roth noticed someone else was there. A woman in a sprigged muslin walking dress stood near the riverbank, a bonnet obscuring her features. But since she wasn't a maid, Roth had to presume it was Mrs. Dunthorpe. He certainly hoped it was her.

Taking long strides, he closed the distance until he arrived at her side. She turned her head just as he came abreast of her.

"Lord Rotherham," she said with a touch of surprise. She looked past him. "Did you come alone? I thought everyone was promenading to the river."

He noted she called him Lord Rotherham instead of Roth. Things had not only cooled between them since the Landscape Room, they'd gone frigid. But whose fault was that? He hadn't spoken to her the night after their charged encounter with the lewd painting, and yesterday, she'd been mostly absent. "They aren't far behind me. They stopped at the folly."

"That didn't interest you?" she asked.

"Not particularly. You came ahead of everyone," he said. "I take it the promenade didn't interest you?"

She smiled guiltily. "I arrived outside early and was so enthusiastic about the fair weather that I couldn't wait."

"You are well, then? Lady Cosford said you were feeling under the weather."

"I am quite well today, thank you."

"You were missed yesterday," he said, looking at the river. He didn't want to see her reaction in case she didn't care for his thoughts on her absence.

"That's nice to hear," she responded softly. They fell silent for a moment. He glanced at her from the side of his eye and saw that she too was focused on the water flowing below them.

At length, she pivoted slightly toward him. "It seems we are avoiding each other since the other day. I confess I wasn't ill yesterday. I just needed a respite from the party."

Her bold honesty both shocked and thrilled him. It would have been far easier to go on as they were and pretend as if they hadn't shared a visceral connection. He really didn't think it had been one-sided, but then he hadn't allowed them the chance to know for sure.

He met her gaze, wanting to meet her frankness with his own. "Then I should confess that I was avoiding you after the Landscape Room."

Before he could say more, she said, "That was my impression. Anyway, it's probably for the best." She smiled, but he sensed a tinge of sadness or regret. "You're looking for a new wife, and I have no plans to remarry. I saw you with Mrs. Makepeace yesterday. She seems like she would make a good match. Indeed, I'm surprised you aren't escorting her today."

Roth exhaled after apparently holding his breath. He supposed he was a bit surprised to hear she didn't wish to marry again. And that she was pairing him off with another guest. "I was concerned that I felt too...strongly about you," he admitted, revealing what he'd meant to say after telling her that he'd been avoiding her.

Her delicate, auburn brows arched. "Strongly?"

"I felt an instant connection with you on the first day of the party. I thought you might have felt it too."

"I did," she said softly.

Dammit. He'd suspected it, but to hear her say so made him want to cast all his doubt to the wind and pull her into his arms. However, he could not. "I was concerned that I was being swept away by our mutual attraction instead of focusing on what I need to —finding a mother for my daughters." He looked down and kicked a pebble into the river. "I should not have avoided you, though." Lifting his gaze back to hers, he said, "Please accept my apology."

"You've no need to apologize. I can't disagree that what...sparked between us was rather strong, did you say?"

He nodded, unable to resist smiling. "Yes. And since I am in the market for a wife and you are not shopping for a husband, you are right that it is for the best that we go our separate ways. At least romantically," he added. Besides the physical attraction he'd felt, Roth also liked her. "I hope that we can be friends."

"I would like that. Though, if I'm honest, I might wish we'd kissed the other day. Just once." She flashed a brief smile before turning back toward the river.

Hell. Now she'd done it. She'd said what he'd been afraid to admit even to himself, that if given the chance, he'd go back to the Landscape Room two days ago and kiss her until they both couldn't see straight.

"I regret that too," he whispered, wondering if she could hear him.

She slid a narrowed-eyed glance at him, confirming that his words hadn't been lost on the breeze.

Voices carried to them on that breeze as the others began to arrive. The footman moved to serve refreshments, from cakes and biscuits to ratafia and ale.

Roth was suddenly frustrated as regret tore through him.

"Shall we get ale?" Charlotte suggested. "I understand it's a special batch Lord Cosford requested from his brewmaster just for this occasion."

"Splendid," Roth said with a forced smile, sounding as though he were being squeezed from the inside out.

They joined the others and sampled the ale. It was quite good, and Roth made short work of his first tankard. After the footman refilled the vessel, Roth stepped to the side to stew in his bitterness. Now that he knew the stark truth—that he and Mrs. Dunthorpe not only shared their passion, they regretted not acting on it—he was at sixes and sevens. He unfortunately could not turn back time. But how was he to move forward with this hanging over him?

Dyer's counsel came back to him. Roth did not want to live with regret.

He sipped his second tankard of ale, his gaze rarely leaving Mrs. Dunthorpe. Someone was likely to notice his unabashed focus on her, but he didn't care. He was waiting for something…

And there it was.

She'd moved away from the river in the opposite direction of the path. Where was she going?

Roth stalked toward her and saw that in front of

her was a small break between some shrubs. She was fixated on the ground.

"Did you see something?" he asked.

"A rabbit."

"Perhaps we should look for it," he suggested, his heart stalling in his chest as he waited, breathless, for her answer.

She met his gaze with a smoldering stare. "I think we must."

He grabbed her hand and led her through the shrubbery. A few more feet, and he tugged her behind a tree. Tossing his ale away and dropping the tankard, he snaked his arm around her waist.

"If you truly want to find the rabbit, tell me now," he rasped.

"There is no rabbit."

"Siren," he murmured before pulling her close and claiming her mouth in a blistering kiss.

She curled her arms around his neck and tucked her body against his. He braced her against the tree, clasping her so that their pelvises were locked together.

Her tongue met his as their passion exploded into an incendiary lust. He lost sense of everything except the lush feel of her in his arms, the heat of her mouth, and the sound of her soft moans and whimpers as they kissed.

He longed to remove her bonnet, to thread his fingers through her hair and thoroughly dishevel her. Ravish her. Ensure this was a moment neither of them would ever forget.

As long as he lived, he wasn't sure he could. She evoked a response in him that he'd never experienced, a primal need to own her, to claim her completely—and to be owned and claimed by her.

They broke apart, gasping.

She slid her hands down to the front of his coat. "Have we taken care of that, then?" She sounded as if she'd run from the house to the river.

He wanted to say no. He wanted to say that he wasn't sure they could ever "take care" of anything. He wanted to assure her that he would never stop wanting her, that he would forever imagine how things might have been different.

But she didn't want to wed. And he needed to.

"Yes, I'd say so." The lie burned his mouth like acid.

"Thank you," she said, her eyes glittering. "I shall treasure that—always."

She slipped past him and went back through the shrubbery.

He stared after her, thinking their embrace hadn't improved things. They shared the same sentiment about that kiss, that it was life-changing, and that only made him want her more.

Had he only managed to increase the potential of his regret? One thing was certain: he wanted her even more now than he did before.

Two things. He still didn't want to live with regret.

❧

*T*he encounter with Roth near the river had absolutely put to rest any lingering thoughts Charlotte might have had about leaving. Then she'd come downstairs for dinner and found that Cecilia had seated her and Roth together, which had led to a thoroughly wonderful evening.

And it wasn't over yet.

As the ladies entered the drawing room after dinner, Charlotte waited until the others had landed on chairs and settees, then she approached Cecilia before she could take her own seat.

"May I speak with you a moment?" Charlotte asked.

"Of course." Cecilia walked with her to the side of the room away from the others. "Is aught amiss?"

"I wondered if there was a reason you seated me next to Lord Rotherham this evening."

The glint in Cecilia's eye coupled with her quick glance to the right gave her away. "You hadn't sat next to him yet."

"Try again," Charlotte said with a laugh.

Cecilia fixed her with an expectant stare. "I noticed you were both missing for a short time at the river. *And* I know Roth arrived at the river's edge before the rest of us and that you were already there. That gave you a nice little while to be alone."

"Being alone with someone—with three footmen in attendance—is provocation to seat us next to one another?"

"Your questioning only confirms my suspicion." Cecilia smiled brightly. "I shan't press you for details...yet. I'm just so pleased at the prospect that you —and he—might enjoy one another's company. Even if it's only temporarily."

"I'm glad you talked me into staying," Charlotte said. After missing blindman's bluff, she'd sent Cecilia a note saying she wished to return to Birmingham. That had prompted Cecilia to come and ask why she wanted to leave.

Charlotte had struggled to keep from being specific because she hadn't wanted to tell Cecilia what had happened with Roth in the Landscape Room. Instead, she'd settled for saying the party wasn't what she'd expected.

Aside from wryly pointing out that Charlotte's

departure would create uneven numbers, Cecilia had convinced her that the party and its activities were amusing. She wasn't wrong. Charlotte *had* been enjoying herself—for the most part. She'd just allowed doubt and worry to creep in after Roth had begun avoiding her following their encounter in the Landscape Room.

There'd also been the unsettling conversation with the ladies in the drawing room the day before. Their discussion of motherhood had provoked a sadness that had, in turn, made Charlotte question why she was even here. And that went beyond just this party, though it had been a long time since she'd felt like an imposter. Being in this group of people, perhaps because she didn't know them, reminded her that she was never able to be entirely her true self.

Cecilia touched her arm. "I'm so pleased you decided to stay."

"However, please don't meddle," Charlotte said softly. "I know your family has a history of matchmaking, but please don't feel as if you must match *me*."

"I thought you might consider remarriage after all." Cecilia's brows drew together. "Didn't you say so yesterday?"

Since Cecilia hadn't been in the drawing room when Charlotte had misspoken, someone else must have told her. Hadn't they discussed not sharing information? Or had that just been with the gentlemen? Either way, Charlotte had created her own mess by allowing her mouth to run freely.

"I didn't mean to say that," Charlotte grumbled. "Just please don't play matchmaker for me. I don't want to remarry." She *couldn't*.

"I didn't mean to cause any upset," Cecilia said with concern. "I will respect your wishes, of course.

And I will not suggest that you and Roth partner together for the dancing competition I am going to announce shortly."

Charlotte narrowed her eyes slightly. "What sort of competition?"

"We'll adjourn to the ballroom where there is more space and take a longways form. Then, I thought couples could demonstrate their best steps. It will be rather free and loose." Cecilia's brow furrowed slightly. "Does it sound terrible?"

"On the contrary. It's positively inspired." Charlotte absolutely planned to partner with Roth, and they would demonstrate their Landscape Twirl. "Is there a prize for the best dance?"

Cecilia cocked her head. "I hadn't considered that."

"How can you have a competition if there's no prize?"

"You make a good point. Last year at the party, we had a hunt for items on a list and the winners got to organize the seating arrangement for the following night's dinner."

Charlotte laughed. "That is not much of a prize."

"No, it wasn't, but it was a hasty decision, as I had also neglected to consider a prize for the winners," Cecilia said with a self-deprecating smile. "What do you recommend?"

"The ale this afternoon was quite good. Perhaps you could give a cask to the winner?"

"That is brilliant. I only need convince Cosgrove to part with one." She winked at Charlotte. "Oh, it looks as though the gentlemen are already finished with their port."

Charlotte's gaze shot to the door as the men began to file in. Roth sauntered over the threshold and at first looked as if he meant to come straight to

Charlotte. Then he seemed to register that Cecilia was standing next to her, and he veered in another direction.

Charlotte glanced at her friend, who appeared to be stifling a smile. Her lips practically disappeared as she pressed them together.

When Cecilia's husband entered, she excused herself to join him. Before Charlotte could even look in Roth's direction, he walked toward her.

Charlotte's heart skipped. This...attraction between them was unlike anything she'd ever known. Their kiss had been sublime, and she wasn't sure she believed for a moment that it would be the end of things between them, despite what they'd both said.

Particularly since she'd lied.

That kiss hadn't "taken care" of anything. It had only served to spark an even greater desire, and she hoped they'd have a chance to pursue it before the party ended.

If not, well, then she wouldn't have lost anything either.

"There's to be a dance competition," Charlotte said without preamble as he arrived before her. "In the ballroom. I think we should do the Landscape Twirl."

He laughed. "Do you? Well, I wouldn't want to disappoint you."

Cecilia and her husband then announced and explained the competition, and a moment later, they were all en route to the ballroom. Perhaps not all. It seemed a few people—or, more accurately, couples— had stolen away.

Roth presented his arm, and Charlotte eagerly curled her hand around his sleeve. Once they were in the ballroom, Cecilia directed them into a longways form.

"Oh good, we still have equal numbers," Cecilia said with a wide smile. "And it looks as though Lord Rotherham and Mrs. Dunthorpe shall lead us." She turned to Mr. Goodlands, who was already at the pianoforte.

"Where did he come from?" Roth asked in a low tone.

Charlotte laughed softly, as did the couple— Sir Nathaniel and Mrs. Grey—next to them. "Perhaps there's a secret door."

Roth's eyes danced with mirth. "How enchanting that would be."

"To be clear, there are no rules or requirements," Cosgrove said. "You may demonstrate whatever you think will win. And the prize is sure to be highly desired, for it's a cask of the ale from today's riverside gathering."

This was met with a general approval amongst the guests, particularly the men.

"I hope you mean two casks," Mrs. Wynne-Hergest said. "I'm not sharing mine with my partner."

Everyone laughed, and Cosgrove inclined his head. "One cask each," he clarified. "And now for the dance!" He looked to Charlotte and Roth.

"Ready?" Roth asked.

"I suppose I must be. Goodness, I hope our dance matches whatever tune Mr. Goodlands plays."

Roth gave her a confident smile that heated her blood. "We'll make do."

The music started, and Roth came forward to the middle of the space between them. As Charlotte hastened to meet him there, he called, "The Landscape Twirl!"

He clasped her waist, and Charlotte put her hands on his shoulders. Then they turned in gentle circles while the others talked and laughed.

Charlotte heard:

"What the devil is the Landscape Twirl?"

"I've never seen anything similar to that."

"You made this up!"

"What a scandalous way to dance! I like it!"

Though Charlotte wasn't entirely sure who said what, she was fairly certain the last had been uttered by Mrs. Wynne-Hergest.

"Of course we made it up," Roth responded to one of the comments.

"You should have said making it up as we go," Charlotte whispered. "Else they'll think we conspired."

"Conspired sounds so delicious, doesn't it?"

Thinking that everything to do with him sounded beyond wonderful, she met his green gaze. As they neared the end of the line, she began to feel a bit dizzy.

"How about if instead of twirling our way back, we just do some lively steps? If we don't, we're going to have to do that thing where you hold me very close so I don't get any dizzier."

"I'm afraid I can't refuse such a tempting offer." He pulled her closer and, instead of twirling, guided her back with a series of halting steps, like his minuet, that she managed to follow. "Better?"

"Yes. Until you have to let me go." Their eyes met, and without words, he told her that he didn't want to.

But of course they did. They watched the other dancers who did their best to outdo the Landscape Twirl. Each dance became more elaborate and even ridiculous, and by the end, everyone was crying from laughing so much.

Lady Bradford approached Charlotte, moving between her and Roth. "Your dance with Lord

Rotherham was inspired. However did you manage to come up with that?"

Mrs. Wynne-Hergest joined them. "I think the more interesting question is whether Mrs. Dunthorpe and Lord Rotherham practiced privately." She waggled her brows suggestively and smiled.

"It was based somewhat on the minuet and another dance from Austria." Charlotte looked toward Roth, but he'd was also now engaged with a few gentlemen.

"Time for us to vote!" Cecilia announced.

"Must we?" Mrs. Wynne-Hergest asked. "They were all brilliant."

"If we don't, who's to get the ale?" Sir Godwin responded.

"I suppose we can draw names," Cecilia suggested. "Would that suffice?"

This was meet with cheers of agreement while a few footmen circulated with a tray of wine and spirits. Charlotte watched as the men around Roth took drinks from the tray. Roth hesitated, but then plucked up a glass of port.

Would he excuse himself and return to her? And then what? They'd steal upstairs and surrender to temptation?

Despite the charged nature of their dance, neither of them had changed the rules since that afternoon when they'd proclaimed they were ready to put their attraction behind them.

It seemed the temptation would not go away, so it was up to them to resist.

Charlotte forced herself to turn and leave the ballroom. If all she had from this party were the memories she'd already made with Roth, it would be enough.

It had to be.

CHAPTER 6

*R*oth walked into the card room the following afternoon for the whist tournament hoping to see Mrs. Dunthorpe—Charlotte. He simply refused to think of her in such a formal manner. Not after their embrace near the river and not after the thoroughly lurid dreams he'd had about her last night.

The way they'd been separated after the dancing had been wholly frustrating. And yet, if he'd excused himself from the other men to return to her, it would have been remarked upon. The last thing he wanted —or needed—was for the other guests, especially the gentlemen, to make any assumptions about his...connection to Charlotte.

Particularly when they'd agreed at the river that their kiss had resolved their attraction.

Except, he now desperately wanted to renege on that accord.

He'd had the sense last night as they'd danced that she might feel the same. He would have asked if he'd had the chance. Instead, he'd taken the easy path—a way that might yet be lined with regret.

"Afternoon, Roth," Cosgrove greeted him as he

came into the card room. "Splendid ride this morning, wasn't it?"

"Indeed." Some of the gentlemen had taken a long ride, which had prevented Roth from seeing Charlotte. Which was why he was counting on her being here.

And what will you do with her?

The nagging voice at the back of his head had been asking him variations of that question all day. He knew what he wanted to do: take her in his arms and whisk her upstairs, where he would ravish her and hopefully be ravished in return.

He just needed a firm sign from her that she would be amenable. If she didn't want marriage, would she desire a short, exceptionally torrid affair instead?

Glancing about the room, Roth calculated about half the guests were in attendance. Checking the clock atop the mantelpiece, he saw that the tournament was due to start in a quarter hour. There was still time for her to appear. He only hoped she didn't arrive just as they were sitting down to play.

"I recall you being quite good at whist," Cosgrove said, pulling Roth from the press of his thoughts.

"I haven't played in a tournament for a while, but I do enjoy the game." It required a great deal of strategy, and memorization of card play was key. Roth could lose himself entirely in an excellent game. If Charlotte didn't show up, he'd do just that. The distraction would be most welcome. Hell, it would be welcome anyway. It wasn't as if Charlotte's arrival would magically alleviate his unrequited desire.

That he wasn't sure was unrequited. It certainly hadn't been, and he couldn't believe she'd completely put it behind her, not after the way they'd danced last night.

Roth's gaze drifted back to the doorway, as it had countless times in the past few minutes. His heart leapt. She was there.

Charlotte stepped into the card room, the skirt of her striped muslin gown swaying with her movement. Her stunning auburn hair was simply styled, with a pale yellow band. Curls framed her face, which lit with some emotion as her gaze met his.

Unable to look away, Roth murmured something to his host before moving in her direction, uncaring what anyone thought of his actions or attention to her. Roth drank her in like a lush, delicious port.

She met him partway, moving farther into the room. "Good afternoon."

"I wasn't sure you'd come," he said, smiling. "I'm so pleased you did."

"I enjoy playing whist."

He escorted her to the side of the room, in part to move out of the way, but also to remove themselves to a place where they might not be interrupted by anyone else. "I do too. Perhaps we can be a pair."

"I believe we're drawing cards, but we may get lucky." The corner of her mouth ticked up. "I heard you went riding this morning."

Did she mean him specifically or the men in general? If it was the former, could he hope she was wondering about him—where he was and what he was doing? Those were the things he was thinking about her.

"Yes, Cosgrove guided some of the gentlemen about the estate. I was hoping...the ladies might be there." He'd been about to say he'd been hoping she would be there, but stopped himself lest she really didn't reciprocate his longing.

"I am not much of a rider, so even if we'd been invited, I wouldn't have gone. But I'm glad you had a nice time. I took a walk to the village with Mrs. Grey. We didn't actually make it all the way there. It's farther than we thought."

"Well, I'm glad you're here now. I was sorry our evening ended so early."

She cocked her head. "What do you mean by *our* evening?"

"Just that I enjoy spending time with you. Our dance was particularly pleasing." Pleasing? It was bloody rapturous.

"I thought so too." Her gaze held his, making the moment incredibly intimate. Every time he was with her, he felt this way, as if they were the only people in the world and time could stand still while he looked into her eyes. "I confess I was disappointed that we were separated afterward."

He wasn't wrong, then. She felt as he did. "The party will be over soon."

"Two days left," she said softly.

Roth lifted his hand, reaching it toward her as if he would clasp hers. He wanted to. The need to touch her in some way, even stroking his thumb over her knuckles, was as desperate as any hunger pang or seemingly unquenchable thirst.

"We should make the most of them." Roth didn't want to harbor any regret. Dyer's words were beginning to haunt him.

"It's time to begin the tournament," Lord Cosgrove called from the opposite end of the room from the doorway. "We'll be drawing for pairs and table assignments. If you'll come forward to make your selection, we will begin shortly!"

Lady Cosgrove stood at a table with a bowl filled with slips of paper on which were presumably written their assignments.

"I shall hope we receive identical instructions," Roth said with a heated a stare.

One of her brows gently arched, and she turned, brushing her arm against his. Roth let his hand drift to her lower back, his fingertips barely grazing her gown. He nearly twitched with need.

They moved together to Lady Cosgrove's table. There, Roth gestured for Charlotte to draw first. "After you."

She pulled her paper from the bowl, but didn't read it. Instead, she gave him an expectant look. He drew his own paper, then moved aside with her.

They opened their folded parchment together and showed them to one another. Same table, different pair.

"So close," he murmured with a smile.

"At least we're at the same table," she said, laughing softly.

A few minutes later, everyone took their seats. Charlotte sat to Roth's left. How was he going to concentrate on the game with her so close? Her intoxicating scent stole over him. If he moved his leg a little to the left, he may be able to touch her...

They started play, and things went nearly as badly as Roth could have imagined. He was wholly unfocused and honestly didn't give a damn about the game. In fact, he would be glad to be eliminated so that he could slink away with Charlotte. But that would require her to also lose, and in this first round, one of them had to win.

His attention was also tested by the fact that Charlotte was an excellent player. He couldn't help but admire her strategy. She seemed far more able to acquit herself, despite exchanging the occasional heated glance. And he was all but certain she'd nudged her knee against his at least twice.

Finally, the torture was over. Roth surrendered to defeat, much to the disappointment of his partner, Mrs. Fitzwarren. "I'd heard you were the best player in attendance," she said with a slight pout.

"Whoever said that was mistaken." Roth looked to Charlotte. "Mrs. Dunthorpe outplayed us all."

Indeed, Roth expected she could win the entire tournament, which would be a shame. For then she wouldn't be able to leave and join him upstairs.

Was that what he wanted?

Yes. With every fiber of his being.

Lord Cosgrove announced there would be a short respite before people would draw new table and pairing assignments. Roth stood and moved to hold Charlotte's chair while she rose.

She turned toward him. "Will you stay to watch?"

While part of him wanted to observe her almost certain victory, the rest of him was desperate to retreat to his chamber and hope that Charlotte wasn't as good at whist as she seemed. "I think it's entirely likely you will emerge the winner."

"I'm not sure I agree. I got lucky. I was somewhat distracted."

"Were you? I was as well."

"You didn't lose on purpose?" she asked coyly.

He laughed. "I take my whist very seriously. As much as I like you—and I do—I could not allow myself to give anything less than my very best. Alas, today, my best was sorely challenged."

"I'm glad. Not that you struggled, but that you played honestly. You didn't say if you were going to stay or not."

"I actually think I might retire before dinner." He was taking a risk. "Perhaps if you find yourself with extra time after the tournament, we might share more of each other's company. My room is located in the east wing, just past the portrait of Cosgrove's grandfather seated majestically on his horse. You can't miss it—the painting is rather large and impressive."

She arched a brow. "Does it have a *conversational* folly, though?"

Roth snorted a laugh, then put his hand to his mouth. "Look what you made me do. But you do it better," he added.

The others were drawing their assignments from Lady Cosgrove's bowl again.

"I need to determine where I will be for the next round," Charlotte said.

Roth gently and quickly touched her arm. "Good luck."

"Do you mean it? Or would you rather I lose?" There was no mistaking the flirtation in her question or her heady stare.

He nearly groaned. The urge to drag her from the room as if he were some primal beast was overpowering, but he was a gentleman—in deed, if not in his thoughts. "You should win. I believe you can."

She narrowed her eyes slightly then spun about and walked to draw her assignment.

Roth retreated to the doorway, then watched as Charlotte took her seat at a new table. Her partner was bloody Emerson this time. Jealousy reared up inside Roth, and he nearly stayed.

But there was no need. Charlotte would either come find him later. Or she would not.

Either way, he would put an end to this obsession. He hoped it would be in the manner that would be most thrilling for them both.

~

*R*oth had removed his coat and waistcoat along with his boots and stockings. If nothing else, he would be ready to change for dinner.

He'd also drunk a glass of brandy, paced the room about a hundred times, and thought endlessly about kissing Charlotte. Would she come?

If she didn't, he was strongly considering leaving the party. There was no reason to stay. None of the other women interested him in the slightest.

He would worry about marriage another time. For now, he wanted to revel in the joy of being with Charlotte.

Glancing at the clock, he calculated he'd been here plenty long enough for the next round of the tournament to have finished. She must have won.

But of course she had.

Roth threw himself into a chair near the hearth with a frustrated grunt. Stretching his legs out before him, he tipped his head back and looked at the ceiling.

If he left tomorrow, he'd arrive in Hereford early and would have to wait for his friends who were meeting him at an inn there. After congregating, they'd continue to Wyelands, the country seat of his friend, Baron Warham, near Hereford.

He could just as easily brood in his coach and then in Hereford as here. In fact, it would be preferable since he would not be taunted by Charlotte's presence.

He closed his eyes and tried not to think of her. Except her warm chocolate-colored eyes rose in his mind along with her seductive smile. Another quarter hour, then he was going to find his ease in his hand, dammit.

A knock on the door startled him. His eyes flew

open, and he straightened in the chair. Instead of jumping up, he waited, his breath catching. Had he heard what he wanted to?

There it was again. The unmistakable sound of knuckles rapping on wood.

This time, Roth vaulted from the chair. He was at the door in a trice, pulling it open without bothering to ask who it was.

Thankfully, he was not disappointed.

He couldn't help the smile that felt like it split his face in two. "You came."

She shrugged. "I lost."

"On purpose?" He couldn't see her losing any other way.

He held the door open as she walked into his bed-chamber. His heart, already beating fast, picked up a wild pace.

She turned to face after he shut the door. "If you're asking whether I preferred to play whist or come here to your bedchamber, the answer—for your ears only—is the latter." She looked away from him, her teeth worrying her lower lip. "Though I almost changed my mind before I got here."

Stepping toward her, Roth didn't touch her. Not yet. He was afraid she might yet choose to leave.

"What prompted that?" he asked. "Or, what made you decide to come after all?"

She returned her attention to him. "I enjoy your company. More than I enjoy playing whist, it seems." She sounded slightly bemused, as if she couldn't quite believe that was the case. "It was bold of you to invite me here."

"It was bold of you to come. And I am elated."

"You should understand that I haven't changed my mind about marriage. That is not my goal. How-ever, it is yours."

"Ultimately," he said slowly. "At the moment, I am not thinking of that." He let his gaze move over her as he imagined removing every stitch of her clothing.

"Then what are you thinking of?" Her question was deep and husky, full of want.

"I am wondering if you would be interested in something other than marriage." He lifted his hand, hesitating as he looked her in the eye.

She gave him the slightest nod, but it was all the encouragement he needed. He touched the side of her jaw, his fingers caressing her gently.

"Hmmm." Her eyes narrowed slightly. "I am, in fact."

"And what would that be?" he breathed, his heart racing.

"You."

"How convenient, for I feel the same about you." He moved closer and put his other hand on her waist. He felt the curve of her beneath the layers of her clothing and barely kept himself from falling on her like an animal. "I'm afraid our kisses near the river wasn't enough after all."

"No, it was not. I'm glad we agree." She stepped into his embrace and slid one hand up to his neck, reminding him that he hadn't yet removed his cravat. "I suppose there's only one thing left to do."

"Only one?" He lowered his head as he pulled her tightly against him. "There are countless things, and I am eager to show you all of them."

His lips met hers, and it was like watching parchment catch fire. The spark quickly exploded into a consuming flame, burning bright and hot and fast.

This was what he'd been longing for, a physical connection to go with the other ways they connected —with humor and...emotion. He pushed that from his mind. This wasn't a time to indulge those thoughts. This moment was for pleasure.

Her kiss was deep and heady, a sensual exploration, a prelude of what was to come. Roth splayed his hand against her back, pressing his fingers into her as he cupped her nape with his other hand. She held him similarly, one hand curled about his neck and the other clutching the back of his shirt.

He suddenly felt overburdened with clothing. And she was definitely wearing too much. But he couldn't pull away. Not now. The kiss was too intoxicating, her embrace exceptionally divine.

She moved her hand forward, caressing his cheek, stroking her thumb along his jaw. He moaned softly, desperate for more of her touch.

But it was she who pulled away. She remained in his arms at least. Her eyes were bright, her lips pink and plump from their kissing.

Roth fought to take a breath. "Is something wrong?"

"Before we go any further, I need to understand what this is."

CHAPTER 7

*C*harlotte was nearly shaking with need. And nervousness. It had been a long time since she'd done this. She'd had precisely one romantic interlude since Sidney died.

Roth had appeared alarmed when she'd interrupted their kiss. He was breathing heavily, and his cheeks were gorgeously flushed.

She needed to take this slowly, to be sure they shared the same expectations. "This is just for the party, yes?"

"Yes. Although, if you wanted, we could continue for a few days after. I'll be traveling to Hereford to meet some friends before we continue on to a week-long party at Wyelands. That's my friend Baron Warham's estate. You could accompany me to Hereford."

While she thrilled at the notion of spending more time with him, she failed to see how it would work. "And what shall I do when we reach Hereford? I live in Birmingham."

"I'll have my coach take you home."

"That's rather out of the way. How will you get to Wyelands?"

"I'll go with one of my friends. I'll tell them my coach requires repair or something." He stroked his fingers down her cheek. "Please say yes. Just as yesterday's kiss was not enough, I fear the remainder of this party won't be either."

Charlotte wasn't sure the trip to Hereford would satisfy her either, but it was all she could risk. A handful of days with this man who made her feel things she'd never imagined. It went beyond the physical, for he made her laugh and possessed a number of wondrous attributes. He was a devoted father, a committed member of Parliament, and he was as enthralled by their unique connection as she was.

Could she part from him in Hereford? She would have to. In the meantime, she would delight in feeling wanted. Cherished.

"Yes. Take me to Hereford. But first, take me to your bed."

He closed his eyes briefly, and she sensed relief in him. Then his gaze met hers with a fiery desire. "First, I am going to strip every item of clothing from your body."

"I can't argue with that." She kicked her slippers from her feet, then moved her hands to his cravat. "This is also a hindrance." Plucking the knot loose, she pulled the silk from his neck and tossed it aside. Then she pushed him backward toward the chair. "Sit. Watch."

Arching a brow, he backed up until he met the chair. Then he sank down, his gaze fixed on her. "Will you take your hair down?"

"Do you want me to?"

"Yes," he rasped, the seductive tone of his voice as arousing as any caress.

Charlotte reached up to her hair and began to pull

the pins free, holding them in her hand as she loosened the locks. Typically, she removed them more quickly, but with him watching her, she drew out the act until her hair was completely free of restraint. She shook her head and felt her hair graze the middle of her back.

"Beautiful," he murmured. "Can I get up now?" The question ended on a croak. He sounded tortured. She stifled a smile.

"No." Charlotte deposited the pins on a table and moved a little closer to where Roth perched on the chair. He looked as though he was ready to pounce on her. Smiling, she began to unfasten the front of her gown, starting at the left shoulder, then moving to the right. The front dropped open exposing her stays.

She heard Roth suck in his breath. His attention dipped to her chest, where the tops of her breasts rounded above the edge of her corset. Reaching behind her back, she untied the gown, loosening the skirt. She pushed the garment down over her underclothes and stepped from the muslin.

Carefully, she picked it up and laid it over the back of another chair. From the corner of her eye, she noted that Roth had scooted forward. She was surprised he didn't fall off the chair entirely.

"Patience," she said softly as she moved in front of him, standing closer than she had yet. She pushed the straps of her petticoat from her shoulders and untied the waist so she could step out of that as well. This time, she simply set it aside.

Now, she stood before him in just her stays, chemise, and stockings. A few inches of her legs were exposed between her garters and the edge of her chemise. That was precisely where Roth's gaze was currently fixed.

"Should I stop? It seems as though you might want to remove your shirt at least."

He whipped the garment over his head and threw it to the side. His bare chest was magnificently muscled, with a patch of light-colored hair at the center and a faint trail that led down to the top of his breeches.

It took a great deal of effort not to abandon her efforts at seduction and throw herself at him in earnest. So she grasped for humor to keep things lighter for a while longer. "I'm surprised you didn't tear the fabric in your haste," she said wryly.

"I would like to tear the rest of what you are still wearing, but you'll think me a beast."

"Not a beast. Just very...eager." She took another step so that her legs grazed his. "I need you to loosen my stays. If it's not too much trouble."

"Turn." The single word was a dark, passionate command.

Charlotte twisted about, again moving slowly, tantalizing him. That was her intent, anyway.

She felt him begin to pull the strings, loosening the garment. He worked quickly, at odds with her methodic actions.

When it was loose enough, she turned back around and pushed the corset down over her hips, wriggling her legs until the garment reached the floor. Then she kicked it aside as she'd done with her slippers.

"What to remove next?" she asked. "My chemise? Or perhaps my stockings." Charlotte lifted her left leg and nestled her foot on the cushion next to him. Grasping the hem of her chemise, she pulled it up toward her hips, exposing nearly all of her thigh and barely covering her sex. "Do you have a preference?"

"Good God, Charlotte." He flicked his gaze, which

had been locked between her thighs, to hers. "I can't call you Mrs. Dunthrope any longer."

"No, you cannot." She slid her foot along his thigh. "I'm waiting for your answer."

He put his hands on her garter and quickly untied the silk. "Lift your chemise higher."

She edged it up the barest amount. "Like this?"

"*Tease*," he hissed. "Higher."

Revealing just a hint of her sex, she asked, "How about now?"

He stripped the stocking from her leg and threw it away. Returning his hands to her leg, he skimmed his palms up her thigh. He slid them up beneath the chemise. One gripped her hip and the other stroked the outer folds of her sex.

Charlotte gasped as he drew attention to the fact that she was already swollen and desperate for him, probably wet as well. Now, he moved slowly, teasing her flesh from her clitoris to her sheath.

"What about my other stocking?" she managed to say as sensation cascaded through her.

He guided her bare leg to the floor, then lifted the other to the same position on his other side. "It's a nuisance." In short order, he'd removed the garter and then peeled the stocking away.

"You've let the chemise drop," he said in dark disappointment.

She had as she'd moved to the new position. And as her arousal had risen to a new height. She hiked the garment to her waist, completely baring herself to him. "My apologies."

"I want to feast upon you. Will you allow it?"

Desire throbbed in her sex. "Yes. Please."

He moved so quickly, she wasn't sure what happened. Picking her up, he carried her to the end of the bed, where he tossed her atop the mattress, her backside landing near the edge. He knelt on the narrow bench that was positioned at the end and spread her legs.

She felt his breath on her sex just before his thumb stroked her clitoris, swirling in circles until she moaned. Clutching her chemise at her waist, she tried not to arch into him. His finger moved along her folds, parting them before thrusting gently inside.

Now she did move, lifting her hips as he caressed her from within. He found a delicious spot that promised a wondrous fulfillment. After several thrusts that she met with her own, his mouth took the place of his hand, which he splayed atop her mound, holding her down while he ravished her with his lips and tongue.

In an embarrassingly short time, Charlotte's muscles clenched. She gripped his head as he guided her leg over his shoulder and thrust his tongue deep. He worked her clitoris, pushing her over the edge into a rapturous oblivion.

Charlotte cried out as he clutched him, her hips moving in a passionate frenzy. He didn't leave her, not until she began to calm, her legs quivering around him.

Then he was gone.

Fighting to catch her breath, she pushed up and saw that he was removing his breeches. She sat up and pulled her chemise over her head. As she dropped it over the edge of the bed, he crawled up next to her, moving like a predator who was now going to feast on his downed prey.

Except he already had.

She couldn't help smiling. Grinning foolishly, probably. This was the best day she'd ever had.

"What is so amusing?" he asked, the corner of his mouth ticking up.

"Nothing. I'm merely enjoying myself. I hope you are too."

"More than I can possibly describe." He lowered his gaze to her bare breasts. "You are magnificent." He cupped her, and her breast overflowed his hand as he lowered his mouth to her nipple.

Though she anticipated his kiss, she wasn't prepared for the shock of renewed desire. It was as if she hadn't just found her climax. She was already quivering with need.

Casting her head back, she curled her hand around his nape and held him to her. "I suppose you didn't have your fill."

"I don't know that I ever will," he said, barely lifting his mouth from her breast. He suckled her and used his other hand on her other nipple, rolling and pulling her flesh until she moaned senselessly, her entire body stretched taut.

She reached between them and found his rigid cock. "I need you. Now."

He groaned as she stroked him. "Yes." Leaving her breast, he sat up between her legs, positioning himself at her sex.

She looked up at him to see that his eyes were closed, his face creased with ecstasy. Moving her hand faster, she reveled in her power and in their shared joy of giving and taking.

"If you don't stop that, we aren't going to get to the part we both want most."

"How do you know this isn't what I want most?" she asked saucily.

He cracked one eye open. "I should not assume. Is this how you'd like to finish?"

While the idea of him losing control in her hand

held a delicious appeal, she couldn't deny that she was eager to have him inside her. "Not tonight." She narrowed her eyes as she positioned him at her sheath.

Relief flashed briefly and gently across his face as he put his hand over hers. Together, they guided him into her sex. The moment he began to fill her, she smiled. Their joining felt somehow inevitable, the next chapter in a story that demanded to be told.

He moved slowly until he was completely within her. Then he paused entirely as he gathered her in his arms and kissed her. Lifting his head, he looked into her eyes and stroked her cheek. "Thank you for trusting me."

His words nearly broke her. She considered pushing him away and running to her chamber. But she was too far gone. She did trust him, even if she hadn't been completely honest.

Don't think of that now.

Charlotte closed her eyes and surrendered to his embrace. She wrapped her legs around his hips, and he started to move, thrusting slowly at first. Her body acclimated to him, and though it had been years since she'd done this, the sensations were familiar. There were also, somehow, wholly new. Because of him.

He held her tenderly, but also with a fierce possessiveness that made her clutch him with a renewed fervor. She dug her fingers into his flesh and kissed him as they moved as one.

Gradually, his strokes grew faster and deeper. She squeezed him more tightly with her arms and legs, as if she could pull him into her more securely. As if she never wanted to let him go.

Her passion swelled ever higher with each thrust, carrying her relentlessly toward her climax. He tilted his hips, bringing his groin against her clitoris. She

moaned as she rose to meet him, arching from
the bed.

"Come for me, darling," he whispered next to
her ear.

Charlotte hadn't realized that she'd been holding
on, that she'd been prolonging the pleasure. Now, she
let go, her body tightening in preparation for release.
He thrust hard, filling her completely, and bliss
claimed her.

Crying out, she clung to him as her orgasm rolled
through her in waves. Before she could settle, he
pulled away from her.

When she regained her senses, she rolled toward
him. He lay on his back, his eyes closed, his hand
around his slackening shaft. That had been very
thoughtful of him to leave her.

After another few minutes, he slipped from the
bed, and it sounded as though he were cleaning up.
Charlotte tucked herself into the bedclothes and
folded them back for him in invitation.

He returned shortly and lay down facing her.
"That was worth the wait." He grinned, looking every
bit the satisfied lover.

"You were certain this would happen, then?"

"Not at all. I was *hopeful*. And while I may wish
we'd started this...liaison sooner, I am grateful we
have finally got round to it."

"I am too." She snuggled against him and pressed
a kiss to the hollow at the base of his throat. "I would
prefer to keep this between us." Though, Charlotte
realized she was going to have to tell Cecilia, because
she would no longer require a Cosford coach to return to Birmingham.

"There is only one full day left in the party. You
want to act tomorrow as if we aren't having an
affair?"

She lifted her head to meet his gaze. "I would, if that's all right." It just felt very...personal. "I'd like it to be our secret."

"Well, that certainly gives this a forbidden air," he said with a chuckle. "Does this mean I can find ways to smuggle you into a cupboard or nook tomorrow to steal kisses?"

Charlotte giggled. "I don't see why not."

"Then I am wholeheartedly in favor of secrecy."

"Would you mind if we are the last to depart day after tomorrow? That way, no one will see us leaving together."

"I don't care when we go, so long as we do so in the same coach. You'll have to tell Lady Cosford, though, won't you?"

Charlotte nodded. "I thought of that. She'll keep the secret."

He pulled her against him and stroked her back. "Do you mind if I stay for a little while longer?"

"Not at all." She wished she could ask him to stay forever. But she could not as she was trapped in a situation of her own making, in which she could not marry.

She would relish their brief time together and keep the memories close forever.

~

The final full day of the party had been one of the most blissful that Charlotte could recall. Breakfast had brought the announcement of the betrothal between Lord Audlington and Mrs. Sheldon. It wasn't terribly surprising since they had seemed to become a pair since their blindman's buff kiss, which Charlotte had heard about from several people.

Charlotte hoped that she and Roth had managed to keep their affair secret over the course of the day and throughout the ball, which had lasted quite late. Indeed, the only thing that had broken up the festivities was the fact that they would all be leaving today. And now everyone had gone except for Roth and Charlotte, who'd kept to their plan of being the last to depart so that no one would see them leaving together.

Before they left, however, Cecilia had invited Charlotte to her sitting room so they could spend a few last minutes together. Charlotte walked into the bright, cheerful space on the ground floor. It was more intimate than the drawing room, and indeed, Cecilia looked more relaxed than Charlotte had seen her over the past week. Perhaps because she was reclining on a chaise longue.

Upon seeing Charlotte, Cecilia sat up. "Pardon me, I'm afraid that I find myself exhausted now that everyone has gone. Well, everyone but you and Roth." She smiled warmly and stood, crossing to Charlotte. Taking Charlotte's hand, Cecilia gave her a squeeze. "I'm so very pleased for you."

Cecilia, of course, knew the truth about Charlotte and Roth. It had been necessary to disclose their affair since Charlotte was no longer in need of one of the Cosford coaches to return her to Birmingham.

"Thank you, but this is a temporary...liaison."

"Can you sit for a moment?" Cecilia asked, pivoting toward the settee. At Charlotte's nod, they moved to sit down. "There's always a chance you may change your minds before you reach Hereford. And if not, well, what happens then? Do you simply forget about one another?"

Charlotte would never forget about Roth or their

time together, however brief it would be. "We go our separate ways, cherishing our new memories."

Cecilia did not appear convinced. She gave Charlotte a thoroughly skeptical look, her brow arched high in question. "You may yet fall in love. Then what will you do?"

"We will not." Charlotte would not. And even if she did, there was nothing to be done for it. "Our connection is primarily physical, and it will run its course by the time we reach Hereford." And if it did not, they would simply have to manage their lingering passion.

"I've known Roth longer than you. If he falls for you, beware of his skills of persuasion." Cecilia gave her a saucy wink.

Charlotte could well imagine. As much as she loved Cecilia, Charlotte needed to put a stop to whatever ideas or hopes she had about a permanent match between them. "He won't because I am not what he wants. He is searching for a mother for his daughters, and I have no desire to take on that role." The lie came more easily than she might have anticipated, but what choice did she have?

"But you would make an excellent mother." Cecilia seemed rather crestfallen, her lips parting and then the corners of her mouth dipping downward. "Just look at how you support and guide the young women you welcome into your household."

"That is not motherhood," Charlotte said. "Lord Rotherham needs a mother for his daughters, and that will not be me."

Cecilia's gaze moved past Charlotte toward the door. "There you are, John. I wondered if you'd retired." She laughed softly as her husband walked into the sitting room.

He lowered himself into a chair, looking every bit

as worn out as his wife. "Not yet." He and Cecilia exchanged a wordless communication, only detectable by the slight notch of her chin and the subtle flare of his nostrils. And, of course, the way their gazes met. Charlotte suffered a pang of envy at their obvious intimacy. The truth was that Charlotte would give almost anything to have that—and to be a mother.

Charlotte stood. "I should leave you. Our coach is likely ready."

Shaking his head, Cosford sat up straight in the chair. "It is indeed. I came to tell you and then became completely distracted by my exhaustion. What an awful host I am."

"Nonsense. You've been an impeccable host all week." Charlotte looked from him to Cecilia. "You both have. You've no cause to pretend in front of me. Be as weary as you feel in my company. I am so grateful for your kind invitation. This has been a splendid party."

"It has been our pleasure to have you," Cecilia said.

"And to introduce you and Roth," Cosford added. "He is waiting at the coach for you. That's the other part I was supposed to say." He shook his head again and lowered his gaze to the floor.

"Oh, stop that," Cecilia told him with a laugh. She looked back to Charlotte. "When you get to Birmingham, do send word about your maid, Hilda."

"Yes. I'll do that." Charlotte was certain the girl would be thrilled at the opportunity to work at Blickton.

Cecilia stood and hugged her. Charlotte smiled as she embraced her friend. She really was glad that she'd come, and not just because she'd met Roth.

Cosford joined them, and they all walked to the entrance hall together. The footman opened the door, and Charlotte took her leave while the Cosfords stood arm in arm on the threshold.

Roth was waiting for her at the coach, his Hessians dark and shiny and a stylish hat covering his golden hair. Charlotte's breath hitched. Would she ever grow accustomed to his extraordinary handsomeness? Or the fact that, for now at least, he was hers? She'd wanted someone for so long, and the reality was so much better.

"Ready?" Roth asked as she met him.

"Quite." She took his hand as he helped her into the coach.

She scooted to the far side of the seat as Roth climbed in after her. The coachman closed the door, and Charlotte leaned around Roth to see out the window.

"Look at them holding each other up," Charlotte said with a light laugh. "I daresay they will stagger to their chamber and fall onto the bed the moment the coach lurches forward."

The Cosfords waved as they drove away. Roth chuckled. "I think you're right. But the question is whether they will sleep."

"Ah, you think they will find other activities to occupy them."

"I know I would." Roth bent his head and pressed a kiss behind her ear, then trailed his lips down her neck. "Indeed, I plan to savor every moment we spend together, especially after the torture of keeping my hands off you yesterday."

Charlotte smiled as her body heated beneath his touch. "Mostly. What about the music room?"

He lifted his head to leer at her. "Do you have any complaints?"

As he'd indicated, Roth had found a way to smuggle her into an empty room, where he'd stolen more than kisses. He'd pressed her against the door and lifted her skirts, tormenting her with his hand until she'd come apart, all while working to keep quiet. Thankfully, he'd swallowed her desperate cries of release with a soul-shattering kiss.

"I do not," Charlotte admitted. "Now, how long until we reach Beckford?"

"We'll be there before you know it." He gave her a wicked grin just before his lips claimed hers.

CHAPTER 8

he sun was resting on the horizon, ready to turn in for the night, when the coach drove into the yard of the Oak and Ash coaching inn in Beckford. Roth helped Charlotte down, keeping hold of her hand even after she was on the ground. He couldn't seem to keep from touching her. All during the journey from Blickton, they'd been in close contact. At some moments, they'd been closer than others.

It had been the most wonderful time he'd ever spent in a coach. He pondered whether they could travel to Hereford by way of London. But then he'd arrive after the party at Wyelands had ended. He wasn't sure he cared.

"I chose this inn because it is well known for its culinary excellence," Roth said.

Charlotte tipped her head back slightly as she surveyed the four stories of large coaching inn. "It's quite impressive from the outside."

"How does it compare to your father's inn?" Roth asked.

She glanced at him. "The Horse and Harness is about half this size, and only three stories tall. It's also older—it was built forty years ago by my grand-father. I'd say this one was built within the last twenty years."

"The Horse and Harness is no longer in your fam-ily?" Roth found that a shame.

"No, but the gentleman who bought it was someone my father knew well and trusted."

"That must be comforting. Shall we go inside?"

A lad had come forth to guide the coachman to the stables with the coach and four. Roth exchanged a nod with the coachman before guiding Charlotte into the inn. Dyer, who'd ridden beside the coach-man, followed behind them carrying their small cases, which would provide all they would need for the overnight stay. Tomorrow, they would arrive in Hereford. Too soon. Roth's idea to travel via London had a great deal of merit.

Inside, they stood in a large entry hall with white wainscoting and light blue walls. To the right was the dining room and to the left, a sitting room. A wide staircase, its oak a rich, shiny brown, rose before them.

A young woman raced into the hall from the dining room. She stopped before them and read-justed the white cap atop her dark hair. Now that she was stationary, Roth saw that she wasn't a woman at all. She was no more than a girl, fourteen or fifteen years at most.

"Welcome to the Oak and Ash," she said brightly. "I'm Daphne." She smoothed her hands down the neat gray apron that covered her dark blue gown.

"Good evening, Daphne. We are Mr. and Mrs. Ludlow." Roth had suggested to Charlotte on the way that they should pose as a married couple for the night. She'd agreed and was surprised at how de-lighted he was for them to be husband and wife, even if it was only make-believe. "We are staying the night on our way to Hereford."

Daphne's gaze shot behind them. "And is this your valet?"

"Yes, Dyer will require a room as well."

"Of course. I've a suite for you on the second floor, and there's an excellent room for your valet on the top floor. Just follow me." She turned and led them up the stairs.

"Splendid," Roth said as they trailed her. "Dare I hope that dinner is soon?"

They'd reached the landing on the first floor, and Daphne glanced at them with a decidedly concerned expression. "Er, dinner will be at seven this evening."

Daphne seemed to pick up her pace as she climbed to the second floor and led them to the end of the corridor. She opened a door and gestured for them to precede her.

Roth and Charlotte moved into a well-appointed sitting room.

"The bedchamber is through there," Daphne said, pointing to the left. "And there is an adjoining dressing chamber. You don't want baths, do you?" Her brow creased.

Charlotte stepped toward the girl as Dyer took their cases through to the dressing chamber. "Daphne, do you usually greet guests and show them to your rooms?"

The girl nodded, her gray-blue eyes wide. "I often do, yes."

"Do your parents, by chance, own this inn? Or another family member, perhaps?"

"Yes, how did you know?"

Lifting a shoulder, Charlotte gave her a warm smile. "My father owned an inn. You remind me of myself at your age."

Daphne's eyes rounded into large discs. "Did you ever have to...become the innkeeper?"

"No. Has something happened?" Charlotte asked.

Roth saw the flash of concern in Charlotte's features and that she quickly pushed it away.

"Papa slipped on the stairs this morning. He hurt his back, and the doctor said he must remain abed for at least a week. Mama is away at Aunt Theo's helping her because she had a baby. My older brother Aaron has gone to fetch her, but he won't be back until tomorrow." Daphne took a breath before plowing onward. "Mama does most of the cooking, but Aaron has been taking over—he wants to be a chef in London—and he was supposed to take care of all the meals while she was gone for a fortnight. But now, neither of them are here."

Charlotte nodded sagely. "I see. What are you doing for dinner tonight?"

"Aaron had planned for...I don't even remember." Daphne shook her head, and allowed the worry she was undoubtedly carrying to furrow her brow. "But when Papa fell this morning and they decided Aaron should fetch our mother, he left directions for a simple stew with bread. Except Molly, the scullery maid, has only been here a month, and she doesn't know how to look after such large quantities of food. The stew smells as though it's burned. I can't serve the guests something like that!" As she'd spoken, Daphne's tone had risen, and her speed had increased. Her eyes had also somehow grown even wider.

"Especially since one of them may be an earl!" she added with a note of true distress.

Blast. Roth had sent word ahead to reserve his room. Only now he was here as Ludlow, not the Earl of Rotherham. "As it happens, the earl gave his reservation to me. I should have said so downstairs."

Relief washed over Daphne's young face. "Truly?"

"Indeed. No need to worry about him arriving."

"How many guests do you have eating dinner?" Charlotte asked.

"Eighteen."

"That's a goodly number, but manageable. If you'll allow me to help in the kitchen, I would be delighted."

Roth snapped his attention toward Charlotte. She was going to cook? So much for his plans for a lengthy seduction in a bath. Roth had deduced from Daphne's question earlier and the manner in which she'd posed it that a bath would be a strain. Now that he knew the particulars of her predicament, he could see why.

"You would do that?" Daphne did not appear convinced.

"Certainly. I know what it's like when things happen unexpectedly. Our cook fell off a horse once, and we were without her for a fortnight."

Daphne looked at Charlotte as if she were an angel sent from on high. "Then you know exactly how to help. Oh, thank you, Mrs. Ludlow."

The name jolted Charlotte. She felt guilty pretending to be his wife when she could never actually take that role—if he even wanted her to. Her guilt, she realized, stemmed from not telling him the truth. She'd never told anyone, and for the first time, she was tempted. However, the risk was simply too great.

And what of the possible reward?

Charlotte ignored that question posed from the back of her mind and refocused on the matter at hand: helping Daphne. "Let me clean up from the road, and I'll be right down."

"Yes, of course. Just come through the dining room and you'll find the kitchen." Daphne hurried to the door and turned back briefly. "Thank you so very much."

After she was gone, Charlotte turned to Roth. "I hope you understand why I had to help."

"As you said, you saw yourself in her. I am inspired by your kindness. So much so that I will come with you."

She gaped at him. "To the kitchen?"

"That is where the cooking will happen, I presume."

"What on earth will you do?" She shook her head. "I mean, do you even know what to do?"

"Not entirely, but I have been in a kitchen. Indeed, I have made *toast*." Cook had taught him when he was eight. He'd made it precisely four times since.

Charlotte put her hand to her mouth and stifled a giggle. "Well, then you shall be in charge of the bread." Cocking her head to the side, she sobered. "Are you sure you want to do this?"

"If we are to spend as much time as possible together, it seems I must." At her grimace, he added, "I am happy to contribute whatever I may."

"You surprise me," she murmured. "I keep wondering what you're doing with me, and here you are offering to help in the kitchen of a coaching inn."

He didn't like the implication she was making. "What, you think that's beneath me? That...you're beneath me?"

"I'm the daughter of an innkeeper and you're an earl. You can't pretend we share a common background or place in Society."

Well, he could pretend a great many things, but he understood what she meant. "It has never mattered to me."

94

Her gaze met his, and there was a heavy beat of silence between them. Finally, her mouth rounded, and she uttered, "Oh." Her cheeks flushed prettily before she turned and made her way into the dressing chamber.

Roth followed, intent on doing whatever he could to help. With their time together limited, he would spend every moment he could with her. Even if it meant working in a scullery.

~

*O*utfitted with a gray apron, Roth had listened to Charlotte's recommendation that he leave his coat upstairs. However, the heat in the kitchen made him wish he'd also abandoned his cravat and waistcoat.

After conversing with the scullery maid, Charlotte announced, "We'll do steaks, potted fish, cabbage, potatoes, bread, and…" She looked back to the scullery maid once more. "Is there a dessert?"

"Aaron started a pudding, and it's been steaming the last several hours." The maid inclined her head toward a pot on one of the four stoves.

"Have you been watching the water level?" Charlotte asked as she moved to the stove.

"Er, no?" The maid, petite with dark blonde hair and blue eyes, wrung her hands.

"It's all right, Molly. It may be salvageable." Charlotte gave the girl an encouraging smile. "Fetch some water so I can fill the pot around the pudding."

Molly dashed off, and Roth joined Charlotte. "Is it ruined?" he whispered.

"It may be. In either case, it isn't enough for eighteen guests, so we'll need to make a cake. How are your baking skills?" She sent him a wry smile.

"I suppose cake is similar to toast?" Roth responded with a grin.

"There must be a recipe book somewhere."

"It's over there." A new voice, belonging to a boy, drew Roth and Charlotte to turn toward the entrance to the kitchen from the dining room. He looked to be perhaps ten and sported a thick mop of dark hair that was in need of a trim. "On the shelf in the corner."

"Thank you," Charlotte said. "You are...?"

"Oliver. My sister said I had to come help you." He made a face and stuck his tongue out. "I prefer to work in the stables, but she said I was needed more here. I don't know why. I can't cook."

"Neither can I!" Roth said gleefully. "But I can follow directions. Can you?"

Oliver nodded, albeit sullenly.

Charlotte walked over to him. "I am grateful you are here, Oliver. As Mr. Ludlow said, he doesn't know how to cook either. Whichever of you moves the fastest and accomplishes the most shall have the first slice of cake later."

Oliver narrowed his eyes as he considered her offer. "What kind of cake?"

"I don't know yet." She turned to Roth. "Will you fetch the recipe book?"

Roth went to the corner to grab the book and handed it to Charlotte. "That's one task for me." He gave Oliver a smug look, hoping the promise of competition might encourage him to be more enthusiastic.

"Can I pick the cake?" Oliver asked quickly, snatching the book from Charlotte. "That will be one task for *me*." He notched his chin up at Roth.

Roth swallowed a laugh and noted that Charlotte was doing the same. To her credit, she didn't appear bothered by the boy seizing the book from her grasp.

"Yes, please choose the cake," Charlotte said. "We'll just need to make sure we have the ingredients."

"I don't need to look at the book," Oliver proclaimed. "Savoy cake is my favorite."

"Lovely. Can you see if there is a recipe in the book for it?"

Oliver moved to the worktable in the center of the kitchen and set the book down while he flipped through the handwritten pages. Molly returned with the water, and Charlotte directed her to pour it into the pot until it was halfway filled.

"Shouldn't the water be boiling?" Roth asked.

Charlotte looked at him in surprise. "Yes, but I didn't specify that, and Molly apparently didn't know. You are already proving yourself to be a natural cook, which is more than I can say for myself."

"What do you mean?"

"I, ah, my skills are not best used in the kitchen. Alas, needs must." She shrugged. "We shall manage."

"Perhaps you should switch places with Daphne," Roth suggested.

Charlotte shook her head firmly. "Absolutely not. Daphne likely feels the need to be in charge in her father's absence. I know I would. She would feel trapped here in the kitchen and would fret about what was happening out there." Charlotte gestured toward the dining room.

"You sound as if you're speaking from experience."

"I am."

"A woman who enjoys command. I like that." He wasn't trying to sound suggestive, but realized that's precisely how it had come out.

Charlotte merely arched a brow at him.

"Found it!" Oliver said.

"Excellent." Charlotte moved next to the boy "Can you gather the ingredients?"

He nodded and shot a superior glance toward Roth. Then he took off, presumably for the larder.

Charlotte turned to the maid. "Molly, you are going to try your hand at preparing the cake. I am here if you have questions, and you will need to check in with me periodically as there are several crucial moments including the separation of the eggs and yolks, the mixing of the egg whites, and the combination of all the ingredients to ensure everything is mixed properly."

Molly chewed her lip. "That sounds difficult."

"It can be, but we'll be methodical, and though we are harried, we shan't rush." Charlotte patted her girl's shoulder. "Now, have you been keeping an eye on the bread?"

"What bread?" Roth looked about. "I thought that was my job."

"We would be in trouble if there was no bread started," Charlotte said with a laugh. "It's over there, rising next to that stove."

"How am I to beat Oliver if my job is already done?" Roth asked with a mock pout.

"It will be ready to bake soon, and ensuring it doesn't burn will be *one* of your jobs. I'm going to need you to peel potatoes now."

Roth straightened his spine. "Yes, ma'am. Where do I find those?"

"Go where Oliver went. I'll find you a knife."

Time blurred as they set to work, each of them taking direction from Charlotte. Daphne checked in now and again, providing help as she could.

Oliver had wanted to sear the steaks, but Charlotte had said he was needed to oversee the cabbage so it wouldn't get overcooked to mush. When he'd balked, Charlotte had assured him the cabbage was a much more difficult and therefore important job.

Now, she was helping Roth determine how to season the steaks before they put them in pans over the range, which contained a truly open flame as compared to the stoves.

"My father always sprinkled salt and rosemary on them," Charlotte said.

"Your father cooked?"

"Not often, and when he did, it was just for the two of us." Charlotte's smile was so charming that Roth couldn't look away from her.

"You have such fond memories of him, don't you?"

"I do, and I confess tonight is bringing them all back. I hadn't realized how much I missed him—and this. Well, not the cooking part," she added drily.

They seasoned the steaks and put the first batch into the pans. Roth found a pair of tongs to turn them over. "How long do they cook on each side?"

Charlotte sucked in a breath and puckered her lips while she considered his question. "Until they look done?"

Roth's laugh was interrupted by a yelp of pain from Oliver.

Rushing to the boy, Charlotte asked. "What happened?"

Roth looked over to see Oliver had the side of hand stuffed in his mouth. He mumbled something, but Roth couldn't understand.

"Accidents happen to all of us," Charlotte said before turning her head toward Molly, who was tending the potatoes. "Is there cool water somewhere?"

"On that cupboard over there." Molly pointed to-ward the opposite wall from where Charlotte stood with Oliver.

"I'll get it," Roth said, hurrying to fetch the pitcher.

"Grab a cloth too," Charlotte called as he rubbed Oliver's back in soothing circles.

Roth swept up the pitcher and turned to find a cloth—he thought he'd seen one on the worktable. Moving quickly, he caught his foot on the leg of the table and lost his balance. The tongs and pitcher went flying as he sought to catch his fall.

He heard the clay pitcher break and the tongs clatter on the floor as he landed on his hands. Pain shot through his palms and his knees, which also hit the stone floor.

"Are you all right?"

He recognized Charlotte's voice and that she sounded concerned. "Fine. Sorry about the pitcher."

"I'll get more water," Molly said.

Roth pushed himself up and used the table to brace himself as he stood. He grimaced as he straightened. "That was most inelegant of me."

"Now we're both hurt, so it will be fair again," Oliver said, clearly still focused on winning their competition.

Roth couldn't help chuckling and saw that Char-lotte was again trying not to smile.

Molly returned with another pitcher of water and set it down next to Charlotte. Then she fetched a cloth and gave that to her before rushing back to the potatoes. "Mr. Ludlow, you should check the steaks."

Roth bit back a curse as he made his way back to the stove. Dammit, the tongs were on the floor. He retraced his steps and found the utensil, then froze.

Did he need to clean them? They'd been on the floor. How did he clean them?

"Just wipe them off," Charlotte said, as if she could read his thoughts. She'd wetted the cloth and was now holding it to Oliver's hand while stirring the cabbage.

"There's another cloth over on that shelf near the bowls," Molly said.

Roth swung his head around and saw what she meant. Fetching the cloth, he wiped off the tongs as he made his way back to the steaks. He turned them, worried they would be blackened, but they were not. One looked...dark, but hopefully that would be fine. He was certain he'd eaten a steak that had looked like that.

He only hoped it tasted good. The Oak and Ash was known for its delicious food, and he didn't want to sully their reputation.

Now that he knew the steaks hadn't caught fire, he turned his attention to Charlotte and Oliver once more. She was murmuring something to him, and the boy smiled. Then he was talking to her, something about horses and his father.

Watching them together made Roth smile. She might not be a natural cook, but she looked like she was born to be a mother.

Roth's heart skipped. He hadn't intended to fall in love a second time. Indeed, he was actively against the risk of having his heart broken again.

But the more time he spent with Charlotte, the more smitten he became. Tonight, in this kitchen, watching her in her element and now tending Oliver, it was bloody difficult for Roth to bury his emotions completely.

And yet, he must. Aside from wanting—*needing*—

to protect himself, she'd clearly stated that she didn't want to wed again.

Charlotte's laugh interrupted his thoughts. Oliver was laughing too. She looked over at Roth, and their eyes met. Her laugh faded, but her smile remained.

Was there any chance she'd change her mind about marriage? Dare he even ask?

No, he couldn't take the risk, especially knowing that she was content to remain unwed. He'd already married one woman who hadn't wanted him. He certainly didn't need another marrying him whilst in the throes of their passionate attraction and potentially regretting it later.

That left him with the dwindling time they had left. He would strive to enjoy every moment.

"Roth, one of the steaks is smoking more than is probably acceptable," Charlotte said.

Swearing softly, Roth snapped his attention back to his task. He smiled in spite of it, for he didn't want this night to end.

CHAPTER 9

*C*harlotte finished her last bite of their long-awaited dinner and nearly sighed. It felt so good to be sitting down. And to have eaten. She still couldn't quite believe the man across the table had spent the entire evening in the kitchen of a coaching inn with her.

"Who knew I could passably sear a steak?" Roth sat back in his chair and lifted his wineglass. He took a long sip of madeira.

"It was more than passable." Charlotte dabbed a napkin over her lips and settled back. She too picked up her wineglass for a drink. After swallowing, she added, "This may be the best madeira I've ever tasted."

"It's a Terrantez, which is somewhere between dry and sweet. It's my favorite kind of madeira. I enjoy the rich flavor, and I find it goes well with meat."

"You sound as if you know a great deal about wine."

He shrugged, setting his glass back on the table. "My father had an extensive cellar, and I'm making my way through it."

"Well, it's delicious, and your steak was too."

"It was the rosemary," Roth said with a wink.

She laughed and then shifted her gaze as Daphne, Molly, and Oliver came into the dining room. Molly carried a plate with the savoy cake, which they'd decided not to serve to the guests. Charlotte was concerned it was overcooked and perchance dry. They'd made do with the pudding and found some cakes from yesterday in the larder.

Molly set the cake on the table, and Daphne put down the plates and utensils she was carrying. Oliver slid onto a chair next to Charlotte and yawned. Daphne and Molly sat on Roth's side of table.

"You worked very hard, Oliver," Charlotte said. "Even after burning yourself. I'm proud of you."

He showed her the side of his hand, where a small red line marred his skin. "It barely hurts now."

"I'm so glad." As soon as she'd been able, she'd found a salve on a shelf in the kitchen and applied that. Afterward, she'd assigned him lighter duties.

"Are you ready for the first piece of cake?" she asked him.

His face lit as he stared at her in surprise. "I won?"

"Of course," Charlotte assured him. "You braved your burn and carried on."

"But Mr. Ludlow fell down, and he carried on too." Oliver looked over at Roth, who was smiling at him. They'd formed a bond over their injuries when the dinner had been served to the guests and they'd finally had a moment's peace.

"Yes, well, a burn is worse than a tumble," Roth said. "You've earned the first piece."

"You must have the second," Oliver insisted.

"If Mrs. Ludlow agrees." Roth gave her a teasing glance.

Charlotte arched a brow in response. Cutting the

first piece, she wondered if she'd been wrong about the cake. It didn't seem dry after all. She set it on a plate and put it in front of Oliver.

He picked up a fork, but looked at Charlotte. "Don't worry, I won't take a bite until everyone gets a slice."

"Such wonderful manners," Charlotte said approvingly. She shifted her gaze to Daphne. "You must tell your mother and father."

"Oh, I forgot to tell you that my father says thank you. He is very appreciative of your help, and he insists that you won't pay for your lodging or meals."

"That is exceedingly kind of him," Roth said.

Charlotte handed him a plate with the next piece. Later, she would tell him that they would absolutely need to pay Mr. Jameson.

She cut a third piece and slid it onto a plate. "I'm just pleased the guests were so understanding."

Daphne accepted the serving with a nod. "They were very kind about our circumstances. I was concerned there was a lady who would be upset that we didn't have as many dishes as usual. But she didn't complain. Perhaps that was because she was too busy drinking the madeira."

"I should think so," Roth said with a chuckle. "It's almost shamefully good. I daresay we could have served them straw from the stable, and the wine would have made it acceptable."

After sliding a plate of cake to Molly, Charlotte cut her own slice, and everyone tucked in.

There was silence for a moment as they all tasted their first bite. "This isn't dry at all," Roth said, cutting another bite with the side of his fork. "It's delicious."

Molly nodded. "It is." She sounded thoroughly astonished.

"You did an excellent job beating the egg whites." Charlotte had thought she would need to help, but Molly had demonstrated a surprising strength and agility for a girl of her slight stature. She'd moved about the kitchen with speed and purpose, growing more confident as the evening had worn on.

Charlotte met Daphne's gaze. "Be sure to tell your parents how wonderfully Molly did tonight. She'll be an asset to you for a long time to come." Charlotte smiled at the young maid, who blushed profusely, then busied herself eating cake.

"May I have another slice?" Oliver asked.

Roth was staring at his plate. "You're done already?"

"Oh dear, I should have told you not to eat so fast," Charlotte said. "Wait a few minutes, and if you still want more, you may have another *small* slice."

She'd expected him to argue, but he nodded and scooped up one last crumb with his fork.

Daphne and Molly finished their cake, and Daphne stood. "Come, let us leave the Ludlows in peace. They are our guests, after all. Oliver, you can have more cake in the kitchen, if you like. But you must carry the dirty forks."

He jumped up to do her bidding and scurried off toward the kitchen. Molly took the cake, and Daphne picked up their three plates—Charlotte and Roth were still eating.

"You've somehow made an impression on him in the space of one evening," Daphne said. "I wish you could stay." She smiled at Charlotte, then took herself off, leaving them alone.

As soon as Daphne was gone, Charlotte looked over at Roth. "You'll need to pay Mr. Jameson anyway. Innkeeping is not as profitable as one would think, not without charging exorbitant prices, which many innkeepers do."

"Your father didn't do that, I'd wager." Roth took the last bite of his cake and set his plate to the side.

"He did not. Nor did he add water to the ale or reheat food from the day before. Cakes, notwithstanding," she added with a smile, lest he think it was wrong of Mr. Jameson to keep food from yesterday.

"I thought the cakes were delicious." Roth and Oliver had gamely volunteered to sample them to ensure they would be acceptable for the guests.

"Yes, there are some things that can be served the next day, but reheating fish, for example, is not something we would do."

Roth wrinkled his nose. "That doesn't sound appetizing. What would you do with food that wasn't eaten?"

"Well, some nights we had bigger feasts than others, as our meals were generally based on what was available in the larder. It's a challenge to have and prepare enough food for your guests while also not creating too much waste. Or any waste, really. It all affects the revenue of the inn. This is why you need to pay Mr. Jameson for our stay." She realized that sounded demanding, and she could not—*would* not—make any demands of Roth. "Or I can pay."

"Heavens, no." He sounded almost horrified at the notion of her paying. "I find myself wondering why you didn't take over running your father's inn when he became ill."

"I was too young, just seventeen. And I needed to care for him. We moved to a small cottage meant for the curate at the vicarage. There was no curate at the time, and the vicar invited us to live there during my father's decline."

Roth's features softened. "That was kind of the vicar."

"He was exceedingly kind and generous. And given that I'd spent so much time with him on my studies, he really was like family."

"Your father was smart—and good—to ensure you had that. He sounds like a wonderful man."

"I was certainly lucky. Well, until he died when I was eighteen." The pain of losing him was distant more than ten years later, but it remained within her and probably always would. She felt more of an ache instead of a deep, crushing agony. She realized, however, that she still felt alone. "I went to live with the vicar after that, and his primary goal was to see me wed."

"And that is what happened, yes?"

Charlotte looked down at her plate and cut another bite of cake with her fork even though she didn't really want any more. "Yes." She put the bite in her mouth so she wouldn't say more. What could she say? That she'd become infatuated with and betrothed to a gentleman only to have him die of an infected cut on his leg a few days before they were to be wed?

How lovely it would be to reveal the truth, but then where would she be after exposing the lie her life had been the last decade?

"What happened to your husband?" Roth asked, his gaze intent—and caring.

She longed to confide in him, but what would be the point? Swallowing the cake, she pushed her plate aside. "He died not long after we wed. I decided it was best to start over somewhere new, so I moved to Birmingham. What happened to your wife?" She asked the question to deflect the conversation from herself, but she truly wanted to know.

Now Roth was the one to look away from her. He shifted in his chair. Had she appeared as uncomfortable when he'd asked about her husband?

"I loved her very much, but she, ah, did not return the sentiment. She suffered from a short illness and died. It was difficult for our daughters, but it's been five years, and I don't think they remember her very much."

Charlotte found that sad, but before she could offer sympathy, he said, "You should have been a mother. You seem natural to the role."

His words seared into her and shot straight to her heart. Her throat constricted. She didn't think she could speak. So she yawned and swiftly raised her hand to cover her mouth.

"You're exhausted," he said, before finishing the rest of his wine. "We should go to bed."

"You must be too," Charlotte responded. "Tired, I mean. Do we need to rise terribly early to get to Hereford?"

"Not terribly. If the weather holds, it should be an easy drive."

Charlotte drank the remainder of her wine, then stood. Before she could pick up her plate, Roth grabbed it and stacked it with his own.

"We can drop those off in the kitchen," Charlotte said.

He nodded, and she preceded him into the corridor that led to the kitchen. A second corridor branched off and led to the innkeeper's suite. Charlotte could only imagine how difficult it was for Mr. Jameson to stay abed while his young children managed things. She wanted to tell him how proud he should be, and that he needn't worry.

Daphne was wiping down the worktable while Molly was making noise in the scullery. Charlotte nearly offered to help them finish cleaning, but she was truly bone tired. Roth took her wineglass and then disappeared into the scullery with the dishes.

Glancing about to see if there was some small chore she could quickly undertake, Charlotte saw that Oliver was slumped over in a chair near the larder. He was fast asleep. Smiling, she walked over to him and wondered if she ought to carry him to bed.

Roth returned and made the decision for her. He swept the boy into his arms and softly asked Daphne where he should take him.

"I'll show you," Daphne said, setting her cloth down and coming around the worktable.

Meeting Charlotte's gaze, Roth said, "I'll see you upstairs."

Charlotte nodded as she watched him follow Daphne back into the corridor. Seeing him cradle Oliver so carefully as well as all the ways he'd pushed and encourage the boy throughout the evening, there was no doubt he was an excellent father.

"Do you and Mr. Ludlow have children?" Molly asked, startling Charlotte.

She turned to fully face the maid. "No, we do not."

"I hope you will." Molly smiled widely at her, revealing a slight gap between her two front teeth. "You'd make excellent parents. You're so happy, so kind and caring. I hope I'm lucky enough to find a husband like Mr. Ludlow someday." The maid returned to the scullery.

Yes, they were happy, but it was temporary. Charlotte felt the impending despair like a weight on her chest. It threatened to steal her breath and render her immobile, both physically and emotionally.

Charlotte would have also hoped she could find a

husband like Roth someday. Indeed, she had found him. And she was going to have to leave him too.

Was there *any* way she could marry him? *If* he wanted to wed her—that was an important detail.

Possibilities moved through Charlotte's mind as she made her way upstairs to their suite. She'd have to tell him everything, and what would that mean for the life she'd led in Birmingham? Would Charlotte Dunthorpe simply cease to exist? She couldn't do that. Aside from her friends whom she'd also have to tell, she couldn't simply abandon her household, particularly the young retainers she was helping and training.

It all sounded too cumbersome. Too draining. And what if everyone despised her, and she ended up truly alone?

None of that took Lord Manthorpe into consideration. She couldn't think of Sidney's cousin without recalling how he'd treated her ten years ago. He'd arrived in town for the wedding a few days before Sidney had died, and Charlotte had met him on two occasions. During both, Manthorpe had looked at her too closely—particularly her chest—and sought reasons to touch her. Then, when he'd called on her at the vicarage the day after Sidney's death to offer his condolences, he'd suggested she become his mistress.

Horrified, Charlotte had refused him, but he'd confidently told her that she would change her mind, and that he'd be more than happy to take her on. Then he'd given her his *card*. As if they'd had a typical conversation that involved some sort of business. It had been offensive and disgusting. Charlotte had taken the money Sidney had given her and left for Birmingham the very next day.

She hadn't told the vicar where she was going,

just that she would write to him. And she had. She'd also exchanged letters with the cook at the Horse and Harness. It was she who had informed Charlotte of Lord Manthorpe's rage upon discovering that Charlotte had left Newark-on-Trent with a large sum of Sidney's money. He'd accused her of stealing it, but Sidney had given it to her as well as left a note detailing what he'd done. Charlotte had no idea what had happened to that note. In hindsight, she should have taken it with her. Or asked Sidney to write another one for her to keep.

Alas, everything had happened so quickly—Sidney's injury when he'd fallen from his horse and cut his leg open on a rock and his subsequent infection. He'd died within a handful of days, which they'd never expected.

Their biggest concern was that Charlotte could be carrying a babe, for they hadn't waited for the wedding ceremony to consummate their impending marriage. But they hadn't been able to wed within the time he'd sustained his injury and died as the final bann had not yet been read. They'd also fervently hoped he would recover.

However, the night before he died, Sidney had summoned her. He'd apologized for possibly leaving her and expressed his concern for her future as an unwed woman with an illegitimate child. He'd made her promise she would go far away and take his name as if they'd wed. Then he'd given her enough money to start her life over and to care for their child. If she'd doubted she could have fallen in love with Sidney so quickly, she didn't after that.

The threat of Lord Manthorpe taking the money Sidney had given her and potentially leaving her and her unborn child with nothing but shame had driven

Charlotte to leave. She would make the same choice today if she had to.

Charlotte had been standing outside her and Roth's suite for several minutes. Blinking, she went inside and made her way to the dressing chamber. Dyer had thoughtfully laid out their nightclothes. The valet had spent his evening helping where he could. He carried cases and trunks for guests and helped to set the table for dinner. Charlotte hadn't spent much time with him, but it was clear he was wonderful, which didn't surprise her since he was Roth's manservant.

As she changed into her nightclothes, she carefully set her garments over one of the pair of racks to keep them from creasing. She couldn't help noticing that Roth's clothing was of a finer quality than hers. It was just another way in which they were worlds apart.

Setting aside her past and the threat of Manthorpe, how could she be a countess? She'd been foolish to even consider it.

Soon, she'd return to her life in Birmingham. Where she was thoroughly content.

But would she continue to be after the time she'd spent with Roth? She couldn't be sure, and that filled her with dread.

CHAPTER 10

*R*oth's back ached from sitting in the same position for too long, but he didn't want to disturb Charlotte. She'd fallen asleep on his shoulder an hour or so ago. He wasn't surprised after their work the night before. After talking with the innkeeper—Mr. Jameson had been most grateful for their help—for some time, Roth had returned to their suite to find Charlotte asleep. He hadn't wanted to wake her, so he'd snuggled her close and joined her in slumber.

But she'd awakened him early that morning, arousing him from sleep and into a pique of desire. It was no wonder she was now asleep once more.

He'd put his hand on her leg some time ago and relished their physical connection as well as the other ways in which they'd bonded. And he did feel... linked to her. He wasn't sure how he was going to let her go.

They would have tonight in Hereford, and then tomorrow, his friends would arrive. He and Charlotte would go their separate ways: she to Birmingham and he to Wyelands, perhaps never to see each other again. Unless they happened to encounter each other at Blickton in the future since the Cosfords were their mutual friends.

Roth wasn't sure he could bear seeing her without being with her.

Perhaps he could arrange to visit her after the party at Wyelands. Birmingham wasn't terribly out of the way of his route home to Ludlow Court, where he would spend a fortnight with Violet and Rosamund before he journeyed to Lune Lodge for his annual hunting party, at which he did not hunt at all.

Stopping in Birmingham to see Charlotte would mean losing time with his daughters, and that was unacceptable. Would Charlotte perhaps want to join him at Ludlow Court? Violet and Rosamund would adore her. After watching Charlotte with the Jameson children last night, Roth was more certain of that than ever.

However, taking Charlotte to meet his daughters was hardly something one did with their lover. Especially when that lover was temporary.

He tipped his head down as much as possible without disrupting Charlotte. He couldn't see her entire face, but he would take every view of her he could get.

The thought of their time together having come down to a matter of hours tore at him. This was what they'd agreed to, but he wanted more. He wanted her.

He loved her.

Closing his eyes, he let the realization burn through him. He'd tried so hard not to feel the emotion, even when he'd known it was coming too close.

But it was too late. His heart was already compromised. Tomorrow, he would be devastated when they parted. So why not take the risk of asking if she might feel the same? Because the risk was whether he could trust himself to *know* her love was real. Pamela had said she'd loved him when she hadn't, and Roth had been completely fooled. Hopefully this time, he'd been more circumspect, more *aware*, of what was actually happening between him and Charlotte.

None of this supposition mattered unless she loved him too and would change her mind about marrying again. Could she say yes to becoming his countess? She would be a wonderful mother to his girls. He had no doubts about that. Isn't that what he'd wanted most? That he'd fallen in love with her was simply his extreme good fortune.

He both anticipated telling her how he felt and dreaded the possibility that she didn't feel the same. Or that she'd just say she did in order to wed an earl. Except, he didn't really believe she would do that. If that had been her intent, she would never have said she wasn't interested in remarriage.

The coach pulled into the yard of the Green Dragon in Hereford. Roth gently stroked Charlotte's cheek. Her lashes fluttered, and she opened her eyes.

"We've arrived, my darling," he said softly.

She lifted her head, and her cheeks were a rosy pink. "My apologies for falling asleep on you. I'm afraid my exhaustion was too much to resist."

"No apology is necessary. You earned every moment of rest. Last night was rather rigorous. As was this morning." He gave her a wicked smile.

Her blush deepened. "You should have been sleeping too. Were you?"

"No, I was too busy watching you, and thinking of you." *And loving you.*

The coachman opened the door, and Roth stepped down, then helped Charlotte to the ground. She faced the three-story coaching inn with its gabled façade. "It looks charming. Do you suppose it could possibly exceed the Oak and Ash?"

"I doubt that, though I daresay it will likely be more relaxing."

They laughed as she took his arm and walked into the inn. As with the day before, Dyer followed them with their cases.

The Green Dragon's entry hall was paneled with rich, dark wood wainscotting and painted, unsurprisingly with bright green. A large painting of a green dragon adorned the wall at the base of the staircase.

There was a coffee room with several tables through an arched doorway on the left. Roth poked his head inside and immediately saw a familiar face. It appeared one of his friends had arrived a day early. That was unfortunate given his and Charlotte's plan to keep their affair secret.

And it was too late to withdraw before the man saw him. His gaze connected with Roth's from where he sat at a table. He stood and strode toward them.

Roth took a deep breath and reasoned it would be all right. He gave Charlotte an apologetic smile. "One of the gentlemen attending the party is already here," he said quietly.

She looked around him, and all the color drained from her face. Damn, Roth hadn't thought she'd be *that* upset.

He put a hand at her back, hoping to comfort her as much as possible in their current situation. "Allow me to present Lord Manthorpe. Manthorpe, this is my friend, Mrs. Dunthorpe."

Manthorpe's nostrils flared, and sharp recognition blazed in his eyes. "Mrs. Dunthorpe, is it? I knew her as Miss Harnessmaker."

"You've met?" Roth looked from Manthrope to Charlotte, who was still incredibly pale.

"Indeed we have," Manthorpe said with a sneer. "Though it's been nearly a decade, I would recognize those lying eyes anywhere."

Lying eyes? What the devil was he about? If it had been that long ago and Manthorpe was calling her "miss," they had to have met before she married. But how?

Roth swallowed and willed his pulse to stop racing. "How did you meet?"

Of course it was Manthorpe who answered. "Shall you tell him? No, I don't think you would." His dark blue gaze fixed on Charlotte, his lip curling.

Manthorpe possessed a temper and a penchant for spite that Roth didn't care for. In fact, Roth didn't particularly consider the man a friend. He was, however, a friend of Warham's, which was how Roth was attending the same party. Manthorpe was part of the group of four who were to meet here tomorrow.

"There's no call to be rude," Roth said, hoping to soothe the fraught moment.

"There is every call to be *honest*," Manthorpe hissed. "She stole a thousand pounds from my cousin when he died, then disappeared completely."

Roth sucked in a breath. "That is quite an accusation, Manthorpe. You must be mistaken. I can vouch for Mrs. Dunthorpe. She is no thief." Roth kept his hand at her lower back. She was stiff as a board.

"How long have you known Mrs. 'Dunthorpe'?" Manthorpe demanded. "Probably not when she was Miss Harnessmaker, the daughter of an innkeeper who'd somehow convinced a vicar to give her shelter, then foist her off on the first gullible marriage-minded male who crossed her path?"

Ice pricked the back of Roth's neck. Manthorpe

seemed to know a great deal about Charlotte. Meanwhile, she continued to say nothing and to look as if she'd been caught, well, stealing.

"Tell him, Miss Harnessmaker, how you stole my cousin's money and disappeared two days after he died."

"We were supposed to be married," she finally said, the words a scratchy whisper as if she hadn't spoken in days instead of minutes.

"But you were not. Sidney died. From a silly cut to his leg, can you imagine?" Manthorpe sent her another accusatory glare. "I've oft wondered how he came to be so ill so quickly. It seems possible, if not likely, that you had something to do with it."

Charlotte's jaw dropped. "You can't think that. I loved him." She shook her head. "It makes no logical sense anyway. If I wanted him to perish, surely it would have been smarter to wait until after we were married when I would have actually been his widow."

"You aren't his widow?" Roth was trying to keep up, but he was woefully lost. And distraught. She'd lied to him? To...everyone?

"No." She didn't meet Roth's eyes, and in that moment, he knew that what Manthorpe said was true.

"Did you really steal a thousand pounds?" Roth couldn't believe she would do that, but if she'd lived a false life for a decade, what had she been hiding? And he would not believe she'd had anything to do with her betrothed's death. Aside from what she'd pointed out, he believed her when she said she'd loved the man. Her "husband."

The realization that she'd lied to him, that she'd never been married at all, hit Roth like a stone.

Charlotte took a deep breath. A bit of color returned to her cheeks. "I didn't steal anything. Sidney gave me that before he died." Now she looked at

Roth, her eyes clear and her expression stoic. "I'm so sorry, Roth. I am not who I said. I regret that I deceived you."

And there it was, another woman he loved who'd lied to him. Once again, he'd let his emotions cloud his judgment. The first time, he never should have rushed things with Pamela. This time, he should not have allowed himself to fall for Charlotte—not when he'd absolutely known better.

"I'll arrange for you to stay at another inn," Roth said woodenly.

She brought her hand to her mouth and inhaled through her nose. Slowly, she lowered her hand. "That isn't necessary. I can make my own way." She turned, but Dyer was not in the entry hall, and neither were their cases.

Manthorpe moved around her to block her way to the door. "You can't leave. Not until you repay what you stole."

Roth's anger surmounted his disappointment. "She doesn't have a thousand pounds in her reticule, Manthorpe. Let her go."

When Manthorpe reached for her, Roth grabbed the man's elbow and hauled him away. "I said to let her go."

Shaking Roth's grip away, Manthorpe scoffed. "I'm going to fetch the magistrate. I'm not letting her get away again."

~

Charlotte couldn't move. This was so much worse than anything she'd anticipated. She'd dreaded Roth learning the truth, but to have him find out like this was beyond horrible.

He'd looked at her in disbelief, then resignation

and finally disappointment, with an additional serving of disgust. Not that she blamed him. She deserved his anger.

Roth, however, didn't deserve any of this. She hated the hurt in his gaze, and the ice in his expression.

"I didn't steal the money," Charlotte said. "Sidney left a note saying he gave it to me."

Something flashed very briefly in Manthorpe's terrifying gaze—guilt perhaps? "There was no note, and you know it. My cousin never would have given you so great a sum."

"Your cousin was a kind, thoughtful man. He didn't want me to be alone without means." She hated voicing the rest, but felt she must. Unable to look at either of them, she cast her gaze to the floor. "He wanted to be sure I was cared for in case there was a child."

"So, you were a whore into the bargain," Manthorpe spat.

"Stop it, Manthorpe."

Charlotte snapped her head up to look at Roth. She'd never heard him sound like that, his voice dark and raw with fury.

"We were betrothed," Charlotte said in her defense, though she really wanted to call Manthorpe out for his scandalous behavior. How dare he question her when he'd tried to persuade her to become his mistress the day after Sidney's death!

"Was there a child?" Roth asked tightly.

She shook her head. "No."

"Then you should have returned the money," Manthorpe said. "Instead, you fled and hid away. Innocent people don't do that. Where have you been? Somewhere poor Roth could find you and be duped, just as my cousin was."

"I loved Sidney, and I love Roth too!" She hadn't meant to speak so strongly or, heavens, to say that she loved Roth just now, but the words had flown out of her mouth unbidden. She hadn't even acknowledged that she loved Roth, and this certainly wasn't how she would have revealed it to him.

Roth wouldn't look at her. "She's been living in Birmingham. We met at a house party."

"And who is Dunthorpe?" Manthorpe demanded. "Another unsuspecting buffoon you used?"

"It's just a name I took."

Manthorpe glowered at her. "I suppose you couldn't use Harnessmaker or Sidney's name, Prewitt, for fear of being discovered."

"Why did you keep hiding?" Roth asked. "After you learned you weren't with child, you could have returned home. Why didn't you?"

Narrowing his eyes at Charlotte, Manthorpe scoffed. "Because she knew she'd have to return the money she stole. Don't be fooled by her preposterous story of my cousin giving her money for a potential child."

Manthorpe was partially right. She couldn't return home because of his allegations—and because he likely would have forced her to become his mistress. But her continued fear of him prevented her from saying so. "What home would I have returned to?" she asked with a dry laugh. "The only home I'd ever known was no longer my home. Was I supposed to go back to the vicarage and endure questions and rumors about why I'd left? Forgive me if I just couldn't do it, if I chose a new start for myself without the ghosts of the past haunting me. Perhaps it was the wrong choice, but I don't regret it." She refused to. Summoning a sliver of courage, she looked at Manthorpe. "Furthermore, Sidney *did* give me that money, and I needed it to live."

"I'll give you a week to repay the funds," Manthorpe said with a condescending smile as if he were doing her a favor.

Charlotte felt as though she'd been dunked in frigid water. There wasn't any way she could repay him that amount. What did he think she'd been living on the past decade? He wouldn't care, even if he *had* thought about it.

She had money saved and invested, and if she sold some things at her house and moved to a smaller residence, she could pay him half now and perhaps make payments. Her mind was swimming, her emotions obliterating any attempt at rational thought. She needed to get away. Where had Dyer taken her bloody case?

"I can't do that," she said, as the walls seemed to close in around her.

"Then I'll have you prosecuted for theft," he said with a sickening glee.

She didn't doubt that he meant it. And he'd probably be successful. He was a viscount, and she was…a make-believe widow.

"Let it go, Manthorpe. Your cousin clearly wanted to protect her, and it was his money to give."

"You've no proof he gave it to her!" Manthorpe railed.

Roth clutched Charlotte's elbow and pulled her outside, slamming the door to the inn behind them. He took a step back from her. "You need to go. Do you need help finding another place to stay?"

She wrapped her arms around herself, feeling suddenly cold. "No, but I need my case and my trunk from the coach."

He looked past her toward the stable. "My coach can still return you to Birmingham."

"I wouldn't want that." She tried to make eye contact, but he wouldn't focus on her. "I'm truly sorry, Roth. I wanted to tell you the truth, but I couldn't think of a way."

"Just promise me you are telling the truth about not stealing that money." Now, he flicked a glance at her, but it was brief—and stinging.

That he doubted her told Charlotte everything she needed to know. There was no hope, not that she'd really harbored any. He would always be an earl, and she would always be the lying daughter of an innkeeper.

"It *is* the truth, and there was a letter. I should have kept it or asked Sidney to write another. He was just so weak by then." Her voice nearly broke, but she wouldn't show Roth the depth of her despair.

Roth nodded. "I'll make sure Manthorpe doesn't pursue you."

That was more than she'd expected and more than she deserved. Even so, she wouldn't refuse Roth's assistance. She only hoped Manthorpe would actually leave her alone. "Thank you."

What an awful way for their joyful affair to end. But Charlotte didn't see how anything could be salvaged. Still, she said, "Perhaps I should have told you the truth, but I hope you can someday understand that I was only trying to protect myself and the life I've built. There are people who depend on me, and I couldn't—" She cut herself off because her reasons probably didn't matter to him. "I realize it must be difficult for you to understand the perspective of a young woman who had no one to ensure she would be taken care of. Sidney tried to do that for me before he died, and I will always be grateful to him."

Roth said nothing; his features were inscrutable.

Charlotte couldn't bear his dispassionate silence. She looked up the street and saw another coaching inn. "I'll inquire about lodging over there. If you could have my things set aside, perhaps in the entrance hall, I'll ensure they are retrieved."

Without waiting for his response, she started walking toward the other inn. Tears blurred her vision, but she blinked them away.

What would she do now? She couldn't really hope to return to the life she was leading in Birmingham. She'd have to start over somewhere else. This time, she'd be who she was—Miss Charlotte Harnessmaker.

A lonely spinster.

~

*A*fter drinking what had to have been his body weight in wine, Roth had collapsed into a dreamless state. This morning, he felt absolutely putrid, and that made him angrier than he already had been. He could hardly wait to unleash his ire on Manthorpe.

Roth cracked an eye open and saw Dyer standing near the bed.

"Good morning, my lord. I've had the cook mix up my redemption cocktail for you."

That was the noxious beverage Dyer insisted Roth drink whenever he overimbibed. Roth hadn't needed it often, but on the rare occasion he did, the stuff had saved him.

"Yes," Roth growled. "Please." He struggled to sit up and grunted with the effort.

Dyer handed him the mug. Holding his nose, Roth downed the liquid as quickly as possible. He handed the empty vessel back to Roth and sank back—slowly —against the pillows.

"You'll feel better soon. Lord Manthorpe asked if you'll be joining him for breakfast, but I informed him you would be dining here." Dyer had heard what had happened. He'd stationed himself under the stairs—not to eavesdrop, he'd said, but to remain close in case he was needed.

Roth closed his eyes as if it could ease the pounding in his head. "He's lucky I don't seek him out and plant him a facer." Manthorpe had strongly resisted Roth's insistence that he leave Charlotte alone. Indeed, Roth wasn't entirely sure Manthorpe would, but he'd threatened the man with social ruin. Roth was infinitely more liked than the viscount, and if Roth gave him the cut direct, his social prospects would wither.

"How do you plan to tolerate his presence at Wyelands for the next week?"

Groaning, Roth opened his eyes. "I don't know."

"Forgive me, my lord, but don't you think there is something you should be doing besides attending another house party?"

Dyer had mostly left him alone last night, but his silence on the topic of Charlotte had told Roth all he needed to know. The valet was waiting to share his disapproval.

Normally, Roth would try to avoid Dyer's lecture, but this morning, he needed to hear it. As upset as Roth had been when he'd learned the truth about Charlotte, he never should have let her go.

His anger had given way to hurt and then his hurt to self-pity. Then he'd surrendered to oblivion. He still pitied himself this morning—because of the sorry state he'd created for himself but not because of Charlotte.

Yes, she'd lied. Not just to him, but to everyone. She'd created a life for herself when she didn't have any other choices. At least, that's how it seemed to Roth based on what he knew.

Roth looked to Dyer. "Yes, there is something else I should be doing. You don't have to convince me."

"Just so I'm certain we have the same thing in mind, what should you be doing?"

"Going to see Charlotte—Mrs. ... never mind—and apologizing."

"I am relieved to hear you say that."

"I should have asked her to stay last night." Roth pushed himself up. "Is there coffee?"

Dyer quickly brought him a cup. "If you'd asked her to stay, would you have then seen her home? I confess I didn't understand the temporary nature of your association. It seems to me that you are well matched. And I haven't seen you that happy in a very long time." He pivoted from the bed and murmured, "Or perhaps ever."

Roth wanted to argue with the man, to say it was an affair and nothing more. But the truth was that he *was* happy. He loved her, and the knowledge of it had given him such joy.

She also loves you too.

Yes, she had said that, hadn't she? He'd been too shocked by the revelations of her past to allow that to sink into his brain.

Hell, he'd made a complete hash of things. While trying to protect his heart, he'd failed to see that his heart could have everything it desired.

He slid from the bed. "I need to get dressed."

"Excellent. Do you want to eat anything?" Dyer asked.

Roth's stomach turned. The concoction Dyer had given him had not yet taken full effect. "Not yet, and I don't wish to wait. The coffee will have to do for now."

"Will you be leaving the inn?"

"As soon as possible. I need to get to Charlotte."

Dyer hastened to the dressing room, and Roth followed as quickly as he was able. God, he'd been an ass.

An hour later, his mood had utterly deteriorated. Upon arriving at the inn where Charlotte had spent the night, he'd been informed that she'd already departed early that morning.

Well, he would follow her. He could make it to Birmingham before nightfall.

After dispatching a note to Wyelands with his regrets to Warham, Roth left Hereford. He'd successfully avoiding seeing Manthorpe, which was the one bright spot in his morning.

Now, as he had hours and hours to brood in his coach, he recalled the events of last evening and desperately wished he'd handled it differently. Charlotte had looked so terrified, so…trapped. He imagined that was how she'd felt ten years ago when her betrothed had died, leaving her unwed and potentially with child.

And that bloody Manthorpe denigrating her for behavior that many people engaged in once they were betrothed. Roth hadn't, but he likely would have if Pamela had wanted to. Of course she would not have. She'd never really wanted to share a bed with him at all.

The pain of that felt somehow less today. Perhaps because he was too upset about Charlotte. Or, mayhap he was ready to finally move on from his former wife and from feeling sorry for himself.

Yes, he'd wallowed in self-pity for far too long. And he'd ensured he wouldn't find the happiness he'd been denied—because he'd been afraid. To withhold himself from love was a ridiculous prospect, and in the end, he'd failed.

Love had found him anyway, and he was so very lucky. He could only hope it wasn't too late to tell Charlotte so.

Would she be angry with him? She ought to be. Would she tell him she never wanted to see him again? He wouldn't blame her. Would she forgive him?

He would fervently hope.

CHAPTER 11

One month later, Lune Lodge, near Lancaster

Since arriving at his hunting lodge three days prior, Roth had spent his time either walking outdoors—alone—or drinking to excess—mostly alone. His intent was to avoid company, but his friends who were attending his annual party had other ideas.

They kept commenting that he seemed morose and inquiring as to his mental state, and none more so than Cosford. His bloody concern had driven Roth to drink far too much last night, and unfortunately, Dyer was not there to ply Roth with his restorative cocktail.

That also meant he was not present to contribute to the barrage of worry. He'd done a fair enough job of that over the past several weeks since Roth hadn't been able to find Charlotte.

Roth opened his eyes and blinked at the bed hangings over his head. He needed cool air. And to stop drinking so much.

But how else was he to manage the pain of losing Charlotte? Or to quiet the near-constant admonishments about how foolish he'd been?

He pushed himself from the bed and went to the dresser on which sat a pitcher and basin. Stiles, his dependable steward who lived at and cared for Lune Lodge, kept the pitchers full of water for Roth and his guests.

After a quick wash, Roth felt at least slightly refreshed. The cool water had eased the ache in his head.

While he dressed, he thought of the awfulness of the past month. Upon arriving in Birmingham, he'd found that Charlotte hadn't yet returned to her house. So, he'd waited. For five days.

Then he'd set off for Newark-on-Trent, wondering if she'd perchance returned to her former home, the one she'd said she couldn't go back to. She had not. However, the people she'd known spoke very highly of her, with love and care as well as sadness for the loss she'd suffered that had precipitated her departure.

He'd stayed at the Horse and Harness and imagined Charlotte bustling about as a girl, helping her father and enjoying a childhood he could only imagine. The inn was beautifully maintained, and everyone there had been incredibly kind and pleasant. Roth knew she would be proud.

If she ever returned. Which she had not during the three days he'd stayed there.

Lost as to what to do next and missing his daughters, he'd returned home to Ludlow Court. Seeing Violet and Rosamund had eased a bit of his heartache, but spending time with them only showed him how wonderful Charlotte would have been as their mother. The girls would have adored her, and now they'd never even meet her. His self-loathing had risen to new levels.

When it came time to leave for Lune Lodge for his annual hunting party at which he did not hunt, he nearly decided not to go. However, Dyer had told him he needed to get past what had happened for his daughters' sake and perhaps the time at Lune Lodge would help him do that.

It had seemed as reasonable a suggestion as any, and so Roth had come to Lancaster and immediately learned that being around other people was a terrible idea. Consequently, he'd tried to keep to himself.

He planned to continue doing just that. Hopefully, in another few days, he'd start to feel better.

Bracing himself for the onslaught of inquisition and cheer if he encountered anyone, Roth made his way downstairs. If he could slip out before anyone noticed...

"Good morning, Roth!" Cosford called from the dining room.

Roth forced himself to the doorway but couldn't summon even a meager smile. "Morning."

"Care to have some breakfast? I ate earlier, but I'm enjoying a cup of coffee. There's no one else here," he added, sounding hopeful.

Damn, Cosford was trying to be a good friend. But Roth didn't want goodness or friendship. He didn't deserve that. He deserved to mope. Alone.

"Thank you for the invitation, but I'm going for a walk."

Cosford jumped up from his chair. "A walk sounds splendid." He brushed his dark hair back from his forehead and came around the table.

Roth wanted to deny him. Perhaps Cosford wasn't ready to depart. Actually, he looked entirely prepared for a walk, almost as if he'd been waiting for Roth to appear and do exactly that. Likely because that was what Roth had done the past two days.

Well, Roth couldn't fault him for being astute. He also couldn't ignore the warmth in Cosford's hazel gaze.

They grabbed their hats from a rack in the entrance hall and made their way outside. The morning was damp and cool, the ground littered with leaves. Nearly bare branches swayed above them in the breeze. It was quiet, and there was an unmistakable hint of the coming winter in the air.

"How are you feeling today?" Cosford asked. He kept his focus straight ahead as they followed a track away from the lodge.

Roth tamped down the instant feeling of irritation the question aroused. In lieu of an answer, he grunted.

"Not much better, then," Cosford said.

"I wish you would stop prodding."

"Did you know that Satterfield left earlier?"

Roth shot a glance toward Cosford. "I did not. What happened?"

"He realized he is in love with the Dowager Duchess of Kendal and has gone to see if he's not too late to tell her so." Cosford couldn't know of Roth's despair or regret, but dammit if this didn't strike Roth square in the heart.

"I see," Roth murmured, feeling positively melancholy. He'd tried to do that with Charlotte, but he couldn't find her. She was very good at hiding, as evidenced by her ability to "disappear" for a decade.

"I've been wondering if your gloom is also due to a matter of the heart."

Roth slowed until he stopped outright. Turning, he ignored how his pulse quickened. "What do you know of it?"

Cosford faced him. "I know you and Charlotte left Blickton together, that you were engaged in a liaison. Can I take your depression to mean that you are sorry the association has ended?"

Sorry didn't begin to describe his emotions. "It's more complicated than that." And Roth didn't want to explain it. He began walking once more.

"As complicated as finding out the woman you might be in love with is not who she purported to be?" Cosford hadn't moved.

Roth nearly tripped. Then he spun around to look at Cosford. His eyes were still warm with kindness and friendship. "How do you know about that?" Roth's thoughts tumbled over themselves. Lady Cosford had been friends with Charlotte for years. Had she known the truth? Had she presented Charlotte to all of them as someone she wasn't.

Did that even matter?

"She's been at Blickton the past month." Cosford grimaced slightly. "I wasn't supposed to tell you. Indeed, I swore I wouldn't. Cecilia is going to be furious with me." He met Roth's gaze. "But I couldn't keep watching you like this."

Why hadn't Roth thought to look for Charlotte there? He moved past Cosford, intent on leaving as soon as possible.

Cosford hurried to catch up with him. "You're going to see her?"

"I have to."

"For the same reasons Satterfield had to."

Roth paused and grabbed Cosford's arm. "How is Charlotte?"

"Not all that different from you. But Cecilia was adamant I not tell you she's at Blickton. She is sometimes accused of meddling when she is only trying to see her friends happy, and Charlotte asked her not to meddle."

"I'm glad you told me. I owe her the biggest apology."

Cosford gave him a faint smile. "I don't think she expects that. She believes you have every right to despise her, that she deserves that."

Roth's heart twisted. To think of how she'd been suffering was like a knife in his chest. She'd been alone and believed he didn't care. Not only that he didn't care, but that he loathed her.

Turning, Roth strode quickly toward the lodge.

Cosford walked beside him. "You're going to Blickton?"

"Without delay."

"What will you do when you get there?"

"Beg her forgiveness. And if I'm lucky enough to receive it, I'll beg her to marry me." She hadn't wanted to wed before. Why would he think he could convince her to do it now? This all seemed hopeless.

Still, he was going to try.

~

Though Charlotte had been home three days, she still didn't feel settled. After the last month, she wasn't sure she'd ever feel that way again. At least not for some time. Being at Blickton with the Cosfords and their children had been a balm, but she was ready to move on with her life.

If not ready, then feeling as though she must. She could not wallow in self-pity forever.

Besides, it wasn't as if she didn't know how to recover from devastation. She knew she could do it.

Why, then, did it seem even harder now than ten years ago?

Because she loved Roth more deeply than she had Sidney. There was a connection between them—she'd been aware of it the moment they'd met. It was why she'd fought so hard to protect herself from him. And why she'd fallen so very hard.

She looked about her sitting room to see what else she could part with. Perhaps the desk would fetch a good price. She could write letters at the breakfast table.

Upon returning to Birmingham three days prior, she'd been met with a letter from Manthorpe demanding she repay the thousand pounds she stole from his cousin.

Again, Charlotte wondered where the letter Sidney had written had ended up. For all she knew, Manthorpe had burned it. Yes, that seemed like something he would do.

She planned to cobble together her savings and sell whatever she could from the house. That would raise about half the funds. Then she would relocate to a smaller residence so that she could make installment payments until the balance was paid. It would likely take her the rest of her life, and she'd have to pare down her household.

She'd also have to stop taking on young women to train in service, such as Hilda who'd come to Blickton while Charlotte had been there. She'd fit in wonderfully, and the Cosfords were delighted to have her.

"Mrs. Dunthorpe?" Charlotte's housekeeper, Mrs. Atherton, stepped just inside the sitting room carrying a candle. An actual widow with graying brown hair, topped with her ever-present white cap, and an exceedingly kind disposition to go with her sharp mind, she was the reason the young women who came to train in Charlotte's household found success elsewhere. "I mean, Miss Harnessmaker. Someday, I won't have to correct myself."

Charlotte had told her household about her true identity and the reason she'd taken on a new name and pretended to be a widow. None of them had cared; indeed, they'd been understanding and supportive. Their only concern was whether she planned to remain in Birmingham. While she'd assured them she would, she hadn't mentioned the need to take smaller lodgings, which would mean finding new positions for half of them. Informing them of that would be the hardest task, and she wasn't quite ready to take it on.

"It's all right, Mrs. Atherton," Charlotte said with a smile. "Do you need something?"

"No, I just saw there was light in here and wondered if it was you."

"Indeed it is." Charlotte could make out the concern in the woman's features in the glow of the candle. "I appreciate you looking in. All is well."

Mrs. Atherton nodded. "I'm glad to hear it. I know this has been a difficult time for you."

The housekeeper didn't even know the half of it. While Charlotte had told them about her past, she'd left out any mention of Roth. What would be the point in discussing him?

"I'm glad to have a moment with you," Mrs. Atherton said. "I've been remiss in informing you of a visitor while you were away."

Charlotte froze. Had Manthorpe delivered his letter in person? Had he bothered Mrs. Atherton?

"It was just a long while ago now—a month or so. Anyway, the Earl of Rotherham called and seemed rather dismayed that you weren't here. He wanted to know where you were, but at the time, I wasn't sure, as we'd expected you back from Blickton."

Roth had come here? A month ago? That had to have been right after he'd learned the truth in Hereford. Her heart sped, and her palms felt clammy.

Mrs. Atheron's brow furrowed as her lips pursed. "Oh, dear, I can see I've distressed you. Please accept my deepest apology for not recalling his visit. I feel terrible about it."

Charlotte knew that around the same time, Mrs. Atherton's sister had been ill. It was no surprise that she hadn't remembered. "I do not blame you in the slightest. Please do not worry about it even for a moment."

"I'll try not to, but you know I will." Mrs. Atherton gave her a soft smile. "I'm off to bed. If I can do anything at all, even if it's just listening, please let me know."

"That is kind of you," Charlotte said. Mrs. Atherton had been with her almost since Charlotte had arrived in Birmingham. Their relationship went deeper than that of employer and housekeeper. "Good night."

"Good night."

After the housekeeper went upstairs, Charlotte decided she should go to bed too, though she doubted she would sleep soon.

Roth had come here looking for her! Why? Did he still want to see her? Should she go to see him? Write to him? Forget they'd ever met?

Charlotte moved toward the entrance hall, which was also the stair hall, and heard shuffling outside the door. She went to make sure the latch was secure. A knock on the door startled her.

Who would be calling at nearly ten in the evening?

"Who's there?" she called. It was her footman's night off.

The door pushed inward—the latch had not caught apparently—and a large figure stepped inside. Fear gripped Charlotte's insides, and when she discerned the identity of the man, it intensified.

Manthorpe stared down at her. His lips curled into a horrible smile. "You have returned at last. I knew it would only be a matter of time, so I've had someone watching for you." He closed the door behind him.

Charlotte stepped back in distress. "You can't just charge in here."

He removed his hat and gloves, then set them on a narrow table. "I've come to discuss repayment of what you stole. You received my letter?"

"Yes." Charlotte swallowed. "I would prefer to discuss this during the day. You may return tomorrow." Honestly, she didn't want him here at all, but she also wanted to do whatever was necessary to get him out of her life.

"Thank you," he said, sounding almost…genial. "I shall return tomorrow as well. However, since I am here now, let us discuss your repayment plan." Manthorpe seized her elbow and pulled her into the nearest room, which happened to be the dining room.

"Release me," Charlotte said, tugging her arm from his grasp.

He squeezed her before letting go. "My apologies. I don't wish to distress you."

She rubbed her arm, relieved he'd released her. Still, she was afraid. How would she get him to leave? "Your demands of repayment for money Sidney *gave* me is distressing. You calling here without an appointment and at this late hour is even more distressing. Please return tomorrow."

His brow creased. "It sounds as though you still

dispute whether you should return the money. That is not debatable. You stole the money. You will repay it, or I will have you prosecuted. There's nothing to discuss beyond the terms of repayment." He stepped toward her. "Now, I would be amenable to an arrangement such as I suggested before, in addition to a cash sum. I find myself in need of funds, so I'm afraid the other arrangement alone would not be sufficient."

Arrangement.

That he'd suggested before.

That could only mean one thing. He expected her to be his mistress. The man was beyond delusional. Her fear took on a sinister edge.

"I am not interested in any sort of 'arrangement.' I am asking you to leave. We can discuss this tomorrow or the next day at my solicitor's office." She did not have a solicitor, but she was damn well going to get one.

He reached out to touch her face, and Charlotte jerked her head back. "Don't touch me," she snapped.

"Uppity chit," he said with soft menace as he grabbed her chin and clasped her arm once more. "I'll do whatever I please, you little thief, and you'll let me, or you'll spend the rest of your days in a penal colony."

Terror tore through her. She had no proof beyond her word that Sidney had given her that money. And Manthorpe, for all his odiousness, was a viscount. No one would believe her over him. "I'll repay you. I've things to sell. I can give you five hundred pounds within the week."

He dug his thumb and forefinger into her chin. "That's a good start. However, I am keen to take my first payment tonight. Where is your bedchamber?"

Tears stung Charlotte's eyes. She was not going to

submit to him. Frantic, she lifted her knee sharply and drove it into his groin.

Releasing her, he staggered backward. Charlotte looked around for a weapon. Her gaze settled on the fireplace set on the hearth. Eyes blurring as emotion overcame her, she dove for the poker.

She grasped the handle and brandished it into the air. And what was she going to do with it? Hit him? That would only worsen her problems.

Vaguely, she realized Manthorpe had been groaning and he'd stopped. She blinked, fighting to regain her equilibrium. He was coming toward her, his face a mask of rage.

She was going to have no choice but to strike him in defense. And she needed to incapacitate him if she had any hope of saving herself. Scaring him would not be enough.

Then she'd have to run again and pray this time she wasn't discovered. Otherwise, she'd end up in that penal colony—or worse.

CHAPTER 12

There was already a coach in front of Charlotte's house. Roth frowned. Perhaps she had a guest. Should he wait until they left? Surely that would be soon given the hour.

Roth's coach drew to a stop behind the other one. Though he ought to wait, Roth found he simply couldn't.

Opening the door, he leapt to the ground and dashed up the short set of stairs to her front door. He took a deep breath to compose himself—or tried to anyway. His heart was thundering with anticipation.

He hesitated. It was a terrible hour to call on someone, especially if they were already entertaining.

Then he heard a shriek and a crash. *Bloody hell.*

Roth pushed on the door and was glad that it gave inward with his weight. Finding his bearings, he saw motion to the left. It was fairly dark, with only a pair of sconces in the entrance all and some faint source of light from where the sound was originating.

Without care, he dashed into what turned out to be the dining room. Two figures were struggling on the other side of the table. He raced around, seeing that it was Charlotte and a large man.

"Charlotte!" he called just before he reached her.

She spun about and slammed into him as he finally saw the face of her attacker: Manthorpe.

"Get behind me," Roth said darkly.

Charlotte slipped around to his back and clutched at his coat.

"What the hell are you doing, Manthorpe?" Roth curled his hands into fists, ready to strike if necessary.

Manthorpe sneered. "None of this concerns you, Rotherham. Kindly see yourself out."

Kindly? Roth wasn't sure what had happened, but Charlotte was clearly afraid and Manthorpe was utterly furious. "You're the one who needs to leave."

"This woman is under my protection," Manthorpe said, much to Roth's incredulity. "I've every right to be here. You're the one who's not wanted."

Charlotte spoke from behind Roth, "None of that is true. I asked Manthorpe to leave."

"We're conducting business, my sweet." Manthorpe spread his lips into a sickly smile.

"Not tonight, you're not," Roth said. "Your presence is not wanted, Manthorpe. Take yourself off before I fetch the magistrate."

"Please do so that I may inform him that Miss Harnessmaker has stolen a thousand pounds from me." He pursed his thin lips as his gaze fell on Charlotte, who'd moved to Roth's side. "I'd hoped we could avoid sending you to Australia, but it appears you are destined for that fate."

Roth put his arm in front of Charlotte, not because he thought she would lunge at Manthorpe—though he wouldn't blame her if she did—but because he wanted the other man to know she was under *Roth's* protection.

"You've no proof of anything," Roth spat. "Charlotte says her betrothed gave her the money, and I believe her. I suspect if we find his manservant and other people who knew him at that time, they would likely support Charlotte's telling of the events. I met a number of lovely people in Newark-on-Trent recently, and they universally adored Charlotte and were sad that her betrothed died. No one found it odd that she left to avoid the reminder of her heartache."

"You went there?" Charlotte whispered.

"Yes," he responded softly. "I'll explain later."

Manthorpe hesitated before jutting out his chin. "We'll just have to see what the magistrate says." His voice held note of uncertainty.

Roth strove to rid them of the blackguard for good. "Let us send for the magistrate, then. I'm sure he'll be interested to hear what you were doing here this evening, uninvited. It sounded and looked to me as if you were making unwanted advances. Indeed, I'm beginning to think I should call you out." Roth didn't dare look at Charlotte, but he slid her a very quick glance. "Did he hurt you at all?"

"No, but he did assault my person and made horrible threats."

"Ah, then honor demands I defend you." Roth narrowed his eyes at Manthorpe. "I shall demand satisfaction in the next thirty seconds if you don't leave—and never return."

Manthorpe sputtered. His inaction spurred Roth into action. Lunging forward, he grabbed Manthorpe by the front of his coat. Then he pushed him around the end of the table where he moved past him and dragged him into the entry hall.

Charlotte had managed to get there too and now opened the door. Roth thew him over the threshold and out into the night. Manthorpe lost his footing and tumbled down the steps.

"Don't come back," Roth warned. "I've a pistol, and next time, I'll use it." He'd fetch it from the coach as soon as Manthorpe was gone. "Furthermore, if you ever harass Miss Harnessmaker again, either in person or by speaking of her to *anyone*, I will find you and I will make sure you never say another word. Do you understand me?"

"I—" Manthorpe gasped as he worked to take in air. "Yes."

"Good. Now get off the street before I call the magistrate. I'll count to ten." He started counting, and Manthorpe leapt up.

Then he threw himself into his coach and the vehicle was moving before Roth reached ten.

"Roth!"

Though he wanted to rush to Charlotte, he first went down to the coach where his coachman, having heard the exchange with Manthorpe, was already fetching the pistol from the box behind the seat. He handed it to Roth. "Here you are, my lord. Shall I stay here in case he returns? I have the other pistol and the rifle, of course."

"Yes, please stay here maybe thirty minutes, then you can go to the mews."

He nodded, and Roth went back to Charlotte's house, closing the door behind him and securing the latch so it was locked. She stood inside the entrance hall and was speaking to a middle-aged woman clutching a candle. Roth recalled the woman was her housekeeper.

"Mrs. Atherton, you likely remember Lord Rotherham. I have him to thank for rescuing me from a dastardly visitor. Roth, this is my housekeeper, but then I gather you meet her some weeks ago."

"In fact, I did. It's nice to see you again, Mrs. Atherton. I do hope you aren't experiencing too much upset from the events that just transpired."

Mrs. Atherton shook her head. "I'm glad to hear all is well. I thought I heard something and then I definitely heard yelling, so I came downstairs. I should have come when I first heard what I thought was a shriek. I convinced myself it was Anna surprised by a mouse."

Charlotte glanced at Roth. "Anna is one of our maids in training."

Roth blinked, feeling a trifle confused now that the danger was past and his pulse was slowing. "Your what?"

"I welcome young women who wish to train as maids into my home. They go on to find employment in other households or even inns."

While he was surprised to hear this, he was not surprised to learn Charlotte did something so helpful and generous. "What prompted you to do that?"

"I knew how fortunate I was to receive that sum of money from Sidney. I vowed I would use it to help not just myself, but others like me—young women who perhaps don't have family support or the ability to choose a future for themselves."

"She's helped dozens of young women," Mrs. Atherton put in. "We've two in training at present." She spoke proudly and smiled warmly at Charlotte.

"Mrs. Atherton is the primary reason we are successful in our endeavors," Charlotte said returning the housekeeper's admiration.

"You are both to be commended. You make me want to do something similar at my house in London. But I would need help. Ideally, that would be someone who has experience." He looked at Charlotte with all the love bursting in his heart.

"I'm going to retreat upstairs now," Mrs. Atherton said. "It's lovely to see you again, Lord Rotherham."

Roth inclined his head toward the charming housekeeper. "And you, Mrs. Atherton."

As Mrs. Atherton disappeared toward the back of the house—presumably to the servants' stairs—Charlotte clasped her hands before her and chewed her lip. She appeared as though she couldn't quite decide what to say.

"Is there somewhere more...comfortable we could talk?" Roth asked. "I came here to speak with you."

"Yes, of course." She pivoted. "I have a sitting room." She led him to the chamber situated behind the dining room, a small but well-appointed and feminine room decorated in pale tones of yellow and coral with a few vibrant touches of red and gold. Whoever had furnished the space had an eye for color without making it feel overwrought. It suited Charlotte perfectly.

She stood in the center of the room, looking as uncomfortable as she had a few moments earlier.

Roth moved slowly toward her, but stopped before he got too close. "Are you all right? That must have been a frightening situation." He studied her face and noticed her chin was reddened. He moved closer. "Did Manthorpe do that?"

She put her fingertips to her jaw, to the right of her chin. "He grabbed me."

She'd said he'd assaulted her, but Roth hadn't really considered the specifics of that. Everything had happened so fast. "I should have called him out. I still can." Fury tore through him. He'd hunt Manthorpe down before dawn. In fact, Roth still held the pistol the coachman had given him.

The touch of Charlotte's hand on his sleeve broke through his rage. "Please don't. I think you scared him away. At least for now. I can scarcely credit the timing of your arrival." She looked dazed.

"I shall thank fate," Roth said firmly, not wanting to think about what might have happened if he hadn't rushed here from Blickton.

"And I will thank *you*." She met his eyes with gratitude and trust. Things he did not deserve after the way he'd treated her in Hereford.

Finally, he was with her. He was suddenly nearly as breathless as when he'd come in to find her struggling with Manthorpe, but in a wholly different way.

"I looked for you," he rasped. "I came here, and when you didn't return, I went to Newark-on-Trent."

"So you said," she murmured. "I can scarcely believe you did that."

"I was desperate to find you. It really is a lovely town, and I meant what I said to Manthorpe. You are loved there—and missed."

She sniffed and pressed her hand to her mouth. "I need to sit down." Wobbling, she made her way to the pale yellow settee with coral-colored flowers.

Roth rushed to help her, but she was already on the cushion. He sat down beside her and set the pistol on a table next to the settee. Though he wanted to take her in his arms and soothe her, he didn't want to upset her. She'd just been practically mauled by another man.

"Can I get you anything? Do you have brandy or something else that might help settle you?"

"That would help, thank you." She gestured to a cabinet. "There should be something in there."

Jumping up, Roth hurried to pour her a glass of

restorative wine. At least, he hoped it would restore her. He brought it to her, and their fingers brushed as she took the glass.

Charlotte lifted her gaze to his, and he would have sworn he saw the love he felt reflected in her gaze. But then, she had said that she loved him in Hereford, hadn't she?

"I was so awful to you in Hereford." He sank down next to her, his leg grazing hers.

She took a long sip of her wine, then set it on the table on the other side of the settee before facing him. "You were shocked and angry, as you had every right to be."

"I should not have let you leave. What sort of man does that?" The shame of his behavior overwhelmed him. "I went to that inn the next morning, but you were already gone."

"I took the first coach I could."

"To Blickton."

"To Worcester, actually. It was there that I decided to go to Blickton. I sent a letter ahead, and Cecilia came to fetch me in Coventry. I didn't want to go home. Besides, I was worried Manthrope might look for me there."

"Which he did tonight."

"He must have had someone watching the house," Charlotte said. "I only arrived three days ago. I'm so lucky you came when you did." Her breath caught, and he saw tears gather in her eyes.

"Oh, my darling, I am too. Please tell me I can hold you. Please tell me I can love you."

Her eyes widened, and one tear slipped down her cheek. "You love me?"

"More than I thought possible. But then, I'd resolved not to love anyone, not after my wife." The pain he typically felt when he thought of her had somehow become almost bittersweet. "I was so in love with her, and I thought she was with me. But when she became ill, she confessed that she'd never loved me at all, that she'd only wed me because her parents insisted upon it."

"She lied to you," Charlotte whispered. "No wonder you didn't want to love again. And then I came along and lied to you too. I'm so sorry, Roth."

"It is not the same," he said firmly. "I understand why you had to lie. I also know that you truly love me. You did mean that when you said so in Hereford?"

Charlotte leaned into him, and he caught her in his arms, holding her tightly. "I *do* love you. With all my heart."

"I feel the same." He kissed her forehead as emotion overwhelmed him. "I love you most desperately. But first, I must beg your forgiveness." He slid from the settee onto his knee and took her hand.

Charlotte shook her head. "There is nothing for me to forgive. I'm the one who should be begging you to forgive *me*."

"There is also nothing for me to forgive. I'm sorry I didn't fully comprehend what you'd gone through when your betrothed died and how quickly you had to make huge decisions that would impact your entire life." He smiled at her. "Honestly, I'm in awe of what you did to protect yourself and what you've been able to accomplish on your own. If I didn't already love you, I would very easily fall."

"You really do understand," she said softly.

"It just took me a little too long." He grimaced. "I deeply regret my behavior in Hereford."

"Let us look backward no longer. I'm just glad you believe me."

"There is no question of that. It is evident to me

that you chose the only path you felt you had, one that your betrothed—and I thank him for it—gave you." He squeezed her hand. "Now, let us look forward. Charlotte Harnessmaker, will you do me the honor of becoming my wife? That is, if you've changed your mind about marriage." He suspected she hadn't, but that she also hadn't been honest about that. If he was wrong, he was going to be bitterly disappointed, for it would mean she really didn't want to wed.

A faint smile curved her beloved lips as she wiped her tears away. "I told you I didn't want to get married because I couldn't, not with this secret. How can they read the banns for an earl's marriage for a woman who doesn't really exist? Sometimes I forget you're an earl. Why on earth would you want to marry me?"

"Why on earth wouldn't I? You're clever, kind, you make me laugh, you appreciate *conversational* landscapes, you love dancing, and you are excellent at running a kitchen even if you aren't the best cook."

She giggled, then quickly sobered. "Are those the things a countess should be? I've no idea, Roth. I wouldn't want to embarrass you. Surely that will happen when they all learn what I did."

"They won't. The moment Manthorpe opens his mouth, his life as he knows it will be over. He won't bother us, especially after you become my countess. That is, if you say yes."

"If they don't learn about that, they will most certainly discover I am the daughter of an innkeeper."

"Probably, and I don't care. They will meet you, like you, and welcome you into Society. How can they not, given your remarkable attributes?"

"Your confidence is both encouraging and daunting."

He squeezed her hand as he moved back onto the settee. "Will you trust me to see you safe and happy?"

"What about your daughters? What if they dislike me?"

Was she looking for reasons to say no? "They will love you as I do." He hesitated, his chest tightening. "Perhaps I've misread things. Perhaps you really wish to remain unwed?"

She pulled his hand fully onto her lap and stroked the back of it with her free hand. "I was devastated when Sidney died. I was already so enamored of being his wife and becoming a mother. As difficult as it would have been to have a child on my own as a fake widow, I was devastated anew when I was not carrying."

"My dearest love," he whispered. "I'm so sorry."

She looked into his eyes with love and something he thought might be hope. "To have the chance to marry and to become a mother is more than I thought I would ever have. It is a dream come true."

"And for me to find someone who will not only be a wonderful mother to my daughters, but who also returns my love is a dream I was afraid to have."

"Then it looks as though we will complement each other." She grinned, and her eyes twinkled. "My answer is yes. I will be your wife."

He wrapped her in his arms and kissed her, softly at first, then with all the passion that had been trapped inside him this past month. She melted against him as she kissed him back, her hands pulling at his shoulders and then clasping his nape.

When they finally separated, Roth smiled. "The first thing I need to do is obtain a betrothal ring."

Charlotte laughed. "The *first* thing? I think the first thing you must do is determine what your coachman is going to do after he delivers your coach to the mews."

"I suppose that's true." Roth chuckled. "He'll come here. Do you have a room for him?"

"Yes. We'll have to wait for him as my footman has the night off. If he'd been here, he would not have allowed Manthorpe in. And before you ask, I was in the process of securing the latch when he pushed his way into the house. I will never make that mistake— not ensuring the door was latched earlier—again."

"I'll be here to protect you." He kissed her again.

A few moments later, when they stopped to catch their breath, she said, "We shall have to delay our retirement to my chamber until the coachman arrives."

"All the more time for my anticipation to grow," Roth said with a suggestive smirk.

She laughed. "I am going to resist the urge to see just how that growth is progressing. On to the next task: what will we do tomorrow? I imagine you'll want to get home to speak with your daughters."

"We will go home—to Ludlow Court—so you can meet them. And so the banns can be read as soon as possible." He pressed his lips together. "I am going too quickly. We haven't even decided where or when to wed."

"I am more than happy with your home and as soon as possible."

"I am relieved to hear that," he said with a grin. He could not keep from smiling. The amount of joy spilling from him was immeasurable.

"I don't know that I want to leave tomorrow," she said with a slight frown. "I need to speak with the members of my household. Oh, Roth, what am I going to do? I can't abandon them."

"There is no reason for you to give up this house if you don't want to. Furthermore, I was quite serious about what I said to Mrs. Atherton. I should like for you to continue your training endeavors at Rotherham House in London. Indeed, we could also offer the same situation at Ludlow Court, though you can't be in three places at once."

"No, I cannot, but Mrs. Atherton can manage this house, and she can train others to do so at your other homes.

"*Our* homes. I can't wait to show them to you."

"I am most looking forward to Ludlow Court because that is where Violet and Rosamund are. I confess I am nervous to meet them."

"Don't be." Roth caressed her cheek. "They will adore you. If Violet could see this sitting room, she'd beg you to refurbish her bedchamber immediately. And Rosamund will delight in everything you'd care to teach her about running an inn. It will contribute to her active imagination. She loves to play make-believe."

Charlotte grimaced, and he realized what he'd said. "That was not meant as anything to do with you. You assumed an identity that you thought was necessary to your survival."

"I know, but thank you for saying that. Perhaps we should leave tomorrow."

"No, I think you had the right of it. We needn't rush. And I won't complain about having another night with you here before we set off into the future."

She cupped his face. "I love the sound of that. But not as much as I love you."

Roth kissed her again and hoped his coachman would arrive soon.

CHAPTER 13

Christmas Eve, Ludlow Court

"*D*o you like it, Mama?" Violet Ludlow asked expectantly. Aged nine, with dark blonde hair and beautiful hazel eyes, she stood next to Charlotte's chair in the drawing room at Ludlow Court.

Charlotte wasn't sure when she'd get used to hearing "Mama" from her new stepdaughters, but it was the most wonderful word she'd ever heard. When she'd married their father a fortnight earlier, they'd instantly called her Mama. It was as if they hadn't just met last month.

Roth had been right when he'd said they would love her. They'd welcomed her openly and with great affection. Charlotte had been incredibly humbled.

The gift from Violet, an embroidered handkerchief, was beautiful. Violet had stitched pink roses, Charlotte's favorite, in the corners. "It is almost too pretty to use," Charlotte said. "But I shall—as often as possible. Thank you, Violet. I love it. But not nearly as much as I love you."

Emotion nearly swept Charlotte away. Roth seemed to realize this as he briefly placed his hand on hers.

"My turn!" Rosamund exclaimed as she thrust a paper at Charlotte.

Carefully taking the parchment, Charlotte set it on her lap atop the handkerchief. It was a drawing of Rosamund's favorite place at Ludlow Court—a small waterfall that emptied into a narrow brook. They'd walked there at least once a week since Charlotte had arrived last month.

"This is wonderful, Rosamund. I love it," Charlotte said, admiring the way Rosamund had captured the water. "Perhaps you should have watercolor lessons."

"*I* asked for watercolor lessons," Violet said.

Roth chuckled. "You can both have them. That's a beautiful drawing, Ros." He looked to Charlotte. "Shall I have it framed for you?"

"Yes, please." Smiling, Charlotte set the gifts on the table beside her chair and held her arms out. "I am so lucky to have such thoughtful daughters."

Violet and Rosamund rushed into her embrace. If that had been the only gift Charlotte received, it would have been enough.

"We need to get ready for tonight's ball," Roth said.

It wasn't really a ball, but they were calling it that for the girls' sakes—especially Violet's. She was incredibly excited about dressing up in a new gown. Rosamund was more looking forward to playing snapdragon and hunt the slipper.

"Come on, Mama," Rosamund said, tugging at Charlotte's hand.

"I'll be up in a moment," Charlotte said, standing. "I need to speak with Mrs. Mallon about a few things." She was the housekeeper, and Charlotte had liked her immediately. Mrs. Mallon had been very curious about Charlotte's training scheme and had even spent a week in Birmingham with Mrs. Atherton seeing how she managed things with the young women she was teaching.

Upon her return, Mrs. Mallon had a plan where she and the head housemaid would oversee training young women from the district. In the new year, Charlotte would continue reaching out to vicarages and poorhouses in the area to establish a path for young women in need of help.

The girls skipped from the drawing room, leaving Charlotte alone with her husband. Who she still couldn't quite believe was her husband.

Charlotte's throat suddenly closed, and she let out a gasp before she could clap her hand over her mouth.

"My darling, what's the matter?" Roth stood and took her in his arms.

"I'm just a trifle overwhelmed. In a good way. I never imagined this is how I would spend my Christmas this year. Newly married. To an earl. With children." She sniffed.

"I couldn't have imagined it either. However, a lovely woman did tell me she hoped I'd find a countess by the new year." He was referring to her, of course, for she'd made that comment the day they'd met at the house party.

"You've Cecilia to thank for that," Charlotte said. "If she hadn't invited us both to that party, we would not have met."

The Cosgroves had come to the wedding, of course, along with Roth's family, including his mother and his brother and sister-in-law and their three children. Some of Charlotte's old friends from Newark-on-Trent had also attended—a few of the people who'd worked at the Horse and Harness and the vicar and his wife. They'd all been delighted to see Charlotte's happiness and promised to speak on her behalf if Lord Manthorpe ever decided to initiate legal proceedings regarding the money she'd been given by Sidney.

Except Roth had repeatedly assured her that he would not. Even Manthorpe wasn't foolish enough to go after the wife of an earl.

Charlotte pulled back slightly to look up at Roth. "I meant to ask if you heard from Manthorpe, though I hate to mention him today of all days."

"I received a letter this morning, in fact. From his secretary," Roth added with a smirk. "The lout couldn't even summon the courage to draft his own correspondence on the matter."

"What did it say?" Charlotte wanted to make sure Manthorpe's accusations and attacks were behind them.

"He congratulated us on our marriage and expressed his confidence that our marriage would be long and peaceful. He wished us every happiness."

"So, he won't bother me anymore?" He hadn't since Roth had thrown him out of her house in Birmingham.

"He'd be a fool to try, and he knows it. No, I'd say we needn't hear from Manthorpe again."

"Except you'll see him in London—in the Lords, at least."

"I'll see him, but I shan't speak to him. He's lucky I don't pummel him into the floor when I next clap eyes on him."

"Thank you for protecting me from him." Charlotte kissed his cheek and made to move away so she could speak with Mrs. Mallon about the order of events for later that evening.

"One moment," Roth said, clasping her tightly against him. "I haven't given you your last present."

"But you already gave me a horse." Whom Charlotte was slightly nervous about learning to ride but was already in love with.

"This is something a bit more personal." He stepped away from her and went across the room, where he pulled something wrapped in paper from behind a chair. As he carried it back, she determined it was a painting.

"What is that?"

"Open it and see." He placed it on the settee they'd been sitting on, leaning it against the back.

Charlotte carefully untied the string holding the paper in place and pushed the wrapping away. It was a landscape. Not just any landscape, but a *conversational* one.

She gasped, then laughed. "Where did you get this?"

"From Cosford's cousin, of course. I asked him to paint something near a river since that was where we first kissed."

Indeed, this was a beautiful landscape of a river with grass and trees in the foreground. The artist's skill had improved since he'd completed the painting that hung in the Landscape Room at Blickton. Up against one of the trees was a woman with her skirts pulled up to her waist and her legs wrapped around a gentleman whose head was bent to her neck where he kissed her.

Charlotte was instantly taken back to that day in the Landscape Room when she'd been so desperate for Roth to kiss her. "I love it. Where on earth shall we hang it?"

"I was thinking in our dressing chamber."

"Behind the door?"

He grinned. "Perfect."

Cocking her head to the side as she studied the painting, she mused, "Why do I suddenly want to go for a walk to a tree?"

Roth groaned as he pulled her back into his arms. "Don't tempt me. Alas, we shall have to settle for a thorough kiss and the promise of later."

"That isn't 'settling' at all," Charlotte said. "It's more than I ever dreamed."

EPILOGUE

Beckford, Summer 1806

*R*oth helped his daughters down from the coach in the yard of the Oak and Ash. Then he took his nearly eighteen-month-old son from Charlotte before he guided her to the ground next.

She reached for James, but Roth shook his head. "My turn."

Laughing, she inclined her head. "Thank you." She held her hand out to Rosamund. Violet had recently decided holding hands was for *children*. "Come and meet the lovely Jamesons."

Since their last visit to the inn, Roth had corresponded with Archibald Jameson. That relationship had turned into a business association when Roth had invested in improvements at the inn. And now Archie was going to expand by opening a second inn in Cheltenham with Roth's financial support.

Roth had never imagined he'd become involved

with innkeeping, but it was something that meant a great deal to him and to his beloved wife.

Daphne, now seventeen and looking like a young woman instead of a girl, rushed from the inn. "Welcome back!" She grinned widely.

Charlotte introduced the girls to Daphne, then gave the latter a fierce hug. "You have grown into a beautiful woman, Daphne," she said softly.

"It's Roth!" Oliver, now fourteen, rushed from the inn. He was home from school, which Roth had eagerly funded. He'd had to work to persuade Archie to allow it, but that had been the beginning of their closer association.

Roth put an arm around the boy as he embraced him. "Goodness, you are very tall. Oliver, meet my son James."

James said, "Bah!" and laughed.

"Are you going to teach him to sear steaks?" Oliver asked.

Roth chuckled. "Not for a while yet. How is Aaron faring?" Roth had invited the young man to Ludlow House to work with his French cook. Aaron was now working in London at a gentlemen's club.

"He's happy, I suppose. He's too busy to write, and I confess I'm not a very good correspondent."

"You'll get better. I recall what it was like to be fourteen. And twenty like your brother."

"Are you going to allow his lordship and his family to come inside?" Archie Jameson asked from the front door of the inn.

"Yes, of course." Daphne gestured for them all to go in.

Roth noted that Violet sidled up beside Daphne, and they began to speak animatedly. He was not surprised that his twelve-year-old daughter would be enamored with a seventeen-year-old.

Allowing everyone to precede him, Roth approached Archie and shook his head. "Hard to believe we haven't seen each other since we met. Through our correspondence, I feel as though it's been more recent."

"Agreed. I'm glad you could come and accompany me to Cheltenham before we finalize the purchase."

"But of course. I've been wanting an excuse to return. My wife and I have very fond memories of the Oak and Ash." Roth stepped into the entrance hall as Archie closed the door with a laugh.

"Working all night to feed my guests is a fond memory? Does this mean you'll be taking over the kitchen this evening?"

Now it was Roth's turn to laugh. "Perhaps not, but we are always eager to help if you need it."

"It's truly good to see you, my lord," Archie said.

"You must call me Roth. If it's good enough for Oliver, it is for you too."

Archie held up his hand. "Fair enough. Why don't you get settled, and then we can have a drink in the parlor?"

"Perfect." Roth followed his family upstairs to a suite of three rooms—one for the girls, a sitting room, and one for him, Charlotte, and of course James.

"Did you really run the inn one night?" Rosamund asked as she sat on every seat in the sitting room. She liked to find the perfect spot.

"We did," Charlotte said. "You should have seen your father bake bread and sear steaks."

"And fall down and break a pitcher," Roth added as he set James down to toddle toward his mother.

"Papa, you didn't," Violet said, sounding horrified.

"I absolutely did. Your mother was the real hero. She ensured everything came off without a hitch."

"Just like she does every day," Rosamund said, settling in a large, squishy chair near the hearth.

"Indeed." Roth couldn't have been more grateful for Charlotte's presence, partnership, and, most of all, love. It was the life he'd dreamed of.

Charlotte scooped James up and nuzzled her nose to his, making their son giggle. Roth went to them and pressed a kiss to the top of James's head as his eyes met his wife's. "Thank you," he murmured.

"For what?" she asked with a perplexed smile.

"For everything."

Thank you for reading The Make-Believe Widow! Check out the rest of the Matchmaking Chronicles, including the prequel, YULE BE MY DUKE, the story of how Lord and Lady Cosford fell in love —reluctantly!

Would you like to know when my next book is available and to hear about sales and deals? **Sign up for my VIP newsletter** which is the only place you can get bonus books and material such as the short prequel to the Phoenix Club series, INVITATION, and the exciting prequel to Legendary Rogues, THE LEGEND OF A ROGUE.

Join me on social media!

Facebook: https://facebook.com/DarcyBurkeFans
Twitter at @darcyburke
Instagram at darcyburkeauthor
Pinterest at darcyburkewrite

And follow me on Bookbub to receive updates on pre-orders, new releases, and deals!

Need more Regency romance? Check out my other historical series:

Rogue Rules
When a young lady is ruined, her friends vow none of them will ever be ensnared by a scoundrel again. They will resist every gentleman's charms even—and especially—if it means gaining a reputation for being impossible to woo. It will take extraordinary rogues to break their rules...

The Phoenix Club
Society's most exclusive invitation...

Welcome to the Phoenix Club, where London's most audacious, disreputable, and intriguing ladies and gentlemen find scandal, redemption, and second chances.

The Untouchables
Swoon over twelve of Society's most eligible and elusive bachelor peers and the bluestockings, wallflowers, and outcasts who bring them to their knees!

The Untouchables: The Spitfire Society
Meet the smart, independent women who've decided they don't need Society's rules, their families' expectations, or, most importantly, a husband. But just because they don't need a man doesn't mean they might not *want* one...

The Untouchables: The Pretenders

Set in the captivating world of The Untouchables, follow the saga of a trio of siblings who excel at being something they're not. Can a dauntless Bow Street Runner, a devastated viscount, and a disillusioned Society miss unravel their secrets?

Wicked Dukes Club
Six books written by me and my BFF, NYT Bestselling Author Erica Ridley. Meet the unforgettable men of London's most notorious tavern, The Wicked Duke. Seductively handsome, with charm and wit to spare, one night with these rakes and rogues will never be enough...

Lords in Love
Six more books by me and Erica Ridley! For those in want of a husband or wife, there is no better time or place to find one's true love than the annual May Day Festival in Marrywell, England. Princes and paupers alike fall head over heels, sometimes with the person they least expect...

Love is All Around
Heartwarming Regency-set retellings of classic Christmas stories (written after the Regency!) featuring a cozy village, three siblings, and the best gift of all: love.

Secrets and Scandals
Six epic stories set in London's glittering ballrooms and England's lush countryside.

Legendary Rogues
Five intrepid heroines and adventurous heroes embark on exciting quests across the Georgian Highlands and Regency England and Wales!

If you like contemporary romance, I hope you'll check out my **Ribbon Ridge** series available from Avon Impulse, and the continuation of Ribbon Ridge in **So Hot**.

I hope you'll consider leaving a review at your favorite online vendor or networking site!

I appreciate my readers so much. Thank you, thank you, *thank you*.

ALSO BY DARCY BURKE

Historical Romance

The Matchmaking Chronicles
Yule Be My Duke
The Rigid Duke
The Bachelor Earl (also prequel to *The Untouchables*)
The Runaway Viscount
The Make-Believe Widow

The Phoenix Club
Improper
Impassioned
Intolerable
Indecent
Impossible
Irresistible
Impeccable
Insatiable

Rogue Rules
If the Duke Dares

The Untouchables
The Bachelor Earl (prequel)
The Forbidden Duke
The Duke of Daring
The Duke of Deception

The Duke of Desire

The Duke of Defiance

The Duke of Danger

The Duke of Ice

The Duke of Ruin

The Duke of Lies

The Duke of Seduction

The Duke of Kisses

The Duke of Distraction

The Untouchables: The Spitfire Society

Never Have I Ever with a Duke

A Duke is Never Enough

A Duke Will Never Do

The Untouchables: The Pretenders

A Secret Surrender

A Scandalous Bargain

A Rogue to Ruin

Lords in Love

Beguiling the Duke by Darcy Burke

Taming the Rake by Erica Ridley

Romancing the Heiress by Darcy Burke

Defying the Earl by Erica Ridley

Matching the Marquess by Darcy Burke

Chasing the Bride by Erica Ridley

Love is All Around

(A Regency Holiday Trilogy)

The Red Hot Earl

The Gift of the Marquess
Joy to the Duke

Wicked Dukes Club
One Night for Seduction by Erica Ridley
One Night of Surrender by Darcy Burke
One Night of Passion by Erica Ridley
One Night of Scandal by Darcy Burke
One Night to Remember by Erica Ridley
One Night of Temptation by Darcy Burke

Secrets and Scandals
Her Wicked Ways
His Wicked Heart
To Seduce a Scoundrel
To Love a Thief (a novella)
Never Love a Scoundrel
Scoundrel Ever After

Legendary Rogues
Lady of Desire
Romancing the Earl
Lord of Fortune
Captivating the Scoundrel

Contemporary Romance

Ribbon Ridge
Where the Heart Is (a prequel novella)
Only in My Dreams
Yours to Hold
When Love Happens

ABOUT THE AUTHOR

Darcy Burke is the USA Today Bestselling Author of sexy, emotional historical and contemporary romance. Darcy wrote her first book at age 11, a happily ever after about a swan addicted to magic and the female swan who loved him, with exceedingly poor illustrations. Join her Reader Club newsletter for the latest updates from Darcy.

A native Oregonian, Darcy lives on the edge of wine country with her guitar-strumming husband, incredibly talented artist daughter, and imaginative son who will almost certainly out-write her one day (that may be tomorrow). They're a crazy cat family with two Bengal cats, a small, fame-seeking cat named after a fruit, an older rescue Maine Coon with attitude to spare, an adorable former stray who wandered onto their deck and into their hearts, and two bonded boys who used to belong to (separate) neighbors but chose them instead. You can find Darcy at a winery, in her comfy writing chair, folding laundry (which she loves), or binge-watching TV with the family. Her happy places are Disneyland, Labor Day weekend at the Gorge, Denmark, and anywhere in the UK—so long as her family is there too. Visit Darcy online at www.darcyburke.com and follow her on social media.